AMAZING GRACE

AMAZING GRACE

A
NOVEL

MALANYA M. DONAHO

AMBASSADOR INTERNATIONAL
GREENVILLE, SOUTH CAROLINA & BELFAST, NORTHERN IRELAND
www.ambassador-international.com

Amazing Grace: A Novel

ISBN: 978-1-64960-054-7
eISBN: 978-1-64960-055-4
Library of Congress Control Number: 2022930975

Editing by Ruthie Walker
Cover design by Hannah Linder Designs
Interior typesetting by Dentelle Design

Scripture taken from the King James Version. Public Domain.

AMBASSADOR INTERNATIONAL
Emerald House
411 University Ridge, Suite B14
Greenville, SC 29601
United States
www.ambassador-international.com

AMBASSADOR BOOKS
The Mount
2 Woodstock Link
Belfast, BT6 8DD
Northern Ireland, United Kingdom
www.ambassadormedia.co.uk

The colophon is a trademark of Ambassador, a Christian publishing company.

To my faithful grandparents,
Ethel White (03/08/26 - 05/10/06)
and
Walter "Ed" White (11/30/24 - 03/05/13),
For their godly examples of what a Christian should be.
I miss both of you, but I'll see you both again.

To my generous mother-in-law,
Who wishes to remain anonymous.
Thank you for supplying the final piece of the puzzle.

To my earthly father,
Larry Moore,
For leading me down the Roman's Road to salvation.

To my patient mother,
Beverly McClure,
For making sure I had a Christian academic education.

To my precocious son,
Gideon Donaho,
For giving me a reason to carry on.

To my loving husband,
Travis Donaho,
For his encouragement and faith in me.
Thank you for giving me the courage to jump.

And to my wonderful Saviour,
Jesus Christ,
For suffering and dying just for me
To pay my sin debt.
Thank You for loving me unconditionally.

CHAPTER ONE

*"But unto every one of us is given grace according to
the measure of the gift of Christ."*

Ephesians 4:7

THE SIX-FOOT-TALL, FORTY-FIVE-YEAR-OLD MAN WITH thick
and short, graying, dark brown hair finished signing his name to the
clipboard and then handed both the clipboard and the borrowed pen
back to the young woman seated behind the four-foot-long folding table.

The blonde-haired woman took the clipboard and pen and said
in a pleasant voice, "If you'll just have a seat, sir, a doctor will be with
you shortly."

"Thank you, ma'am," the man said with a kind smile for the woman
and then turned to survey with searching hazel eyes the twenty folding
chairs lined up neatly in rows that served as a makeshift waiting area
for patients inside the enormous, white medical tent. Since there were
only three others who were waiting to see a doctor, he had his pick of
the chairs, and so he chose to sit on the front row to wait patiently for
his turn. Eventually, he was the only one waiting when he saw a tall,
clean-cut, young man wearing a white doctor's coat over a sandy brown
dress shirt, khaki slacks, and brown sneakers come out into the waiting
area and check with the blonde woman behind the table.

"Thomas Cloverdale?" the young doctor queried in Swahili without looking up.

The man stood to his feet and walked over to where the young doctor was. "Dr. Thomas Cloverdale, that's me," he responded in the same language with a smile on his face as he held out his hand.

The young doctor studied the older man before speaking again, taking the proffered hand and shaking it. "American?" the young doctor asked, this time in English.

"Yes," Thomas answered in a friendly manner, also in English.

"I'm Dr. Sam Gray," the young doctor introduced himself. "I must say, it's nice to hear my own language spoken back to me from one of my patients."

Thomas chuckled in amusement and said, "I understand how you feel, Doctor."

"Follow me, please," Sam said and held open the tent flap for the older man to walk through. Then he began to lead the older man through the tent's "hallways" and into a small room furnished with a cot, some medical equipment, several more folding chairs, and a stool.

"You say you're a doctor, too? What do you specialize in, if you don't mind me asking?" Sam asked the older man.

"Oh, I don't mind at all. My specialty is the heart," Thomas answered.

"A cardiologist, eh? Odd that I don't remember seeing you on the plane with the rest of my colleagues," Sam remarked.

Thomas chuckled and replied, "I'm not that kind of heart doctor, young man. I'm a pastor and missionary." Thomas watched as the young man's smile faded and his body grew tense, but the pastor's smile never vanished, for he was accustomed to this reaction.

"Oh, I see," said Sam, a slight feeling of discomfort coming over him. Sam took the pastor's blood pressure and then, having recovered from his surprise, asked, "So how long have you been here in Africa?"

"Four years now," Thomas answered. "What about you?"

"Just three days but it feels like I've been here forever," Sam said ruefully. "How do you like it here?"

"Oh, I can't complain. The people are so nice and friendly for the most part and willing to learn. What about you?"

"It's hot and dusty, and the patient facilities are deplorable, not to mention the housing situation. The people *are* nice and friendly but they're also starving and malnourished."

"But that's why you're here, right?" Thomas asked the young man.

"I'm here because my boss is paying me, since he receives donations if he sends us to third world countries to provide free checkups to those who can't afford it, all part of a humanitarian aid program."

"'Blessed is he that considereth the poor: the Lord will deliver him in time of trouble,'" Thomas quoted.

"What?" Sam asked in confusion.

"It's Psalm 41:1. You're doing great work here, young man."

"Um, thank you," Sam said. "Now, it says you just need your vaccinations updated; is that right?"

"That's right." Thomas watched as the young doctor prepared the proper vaccines for him. "So, what is your specialty, if I may ask?"

"I'm a general practitioner specializing in pediatrics," Sam answered as he laid out on the metal rolling tray the tools he'd need to administer the shots to the pastor.

"Pediatrics is a noble calling. 'Even so it is not the will of your Father which is in heaven, that one of these little ones should perish.'

That's Matthew 18:14, by the way. Say, you wouldn't, by any chance, be making house calls while you're here, would you?" Thomas asked as he watched the young doctor roll the metal tray over to where he sat waiting for his shots.

"Only for those who can't come here," Sam answered readily as he squirted disinfectant on a cotton ball and then began to rub it vigorously on the older man's upper arm.

"I run a school in addition to my church, and I was hoping that you might come take a look at the children there. Do you think that might be possible?"

"I'd already planned to visit some of the area schools, having obtained their permission in advance, so I don't see why that would be a problem. I will need permission from the parents of the children, however," Sam said and then began to administer the shots one by one.

"You have it already. I'm their primary caretaker."

"There, all done," Sam said. "Now, what do you mean you're their primary caretaker?"

Thomas grinned, pulled out a small piece of paper from his front jacket pocket, turned it over so that the back was visible, and handed it to the young doctor. "It's at the God's Children Orphanage and School. The phone number is right there on the back. You can call and set up a day and time to come out when you're available as well as to get directions. Hours of operation are also listed so you'll know when to call. I really do appreciate this. Medical treatment is expensive, and we have so many children in need."

"I'm happy to help, Dr. Cloverdale. If I can save even one, the time will be well spent."

Thomas smiled warmly at the doctor's words as he stood and put his jacket back on. Extending his hand once again, he said, "'Blessed are the merciful: for they shall obtain mercy.' That's Matthew 5:7. It was a pleasure to meet you, Dr. Gray, and I hope to see you again soon."

"Nice to meet you, too," Sam said and watched the older man leave. Once the pastor was gone, Sam felt his muscles relax again; so, curiously, he glanced down at the paper that the pastor had given to him so that he could get into contact with the school. "'God's Children Orphanage and School, a ministry of the Lighthouse Baptist Church of Africa. Pastor Dr. Thomas Cloverdale,'" he read aloud, noting the hours of operation for the school. It also listed the church's phone number and worship times, but he paid little attention to that. Sam then flipped the little paper over and felt an unexplainable cold chill sweep through him. *Sneaky, old man,* he thought, frowning with disapproval.

In bold, black letters on the cover of the little two-page leaflet were the words "HEAVEN OR HELL? IF YOU DIED TODAY, DO YOU KNOW WHERE YOU WOULD SPEND ETERNITY?"

Dr. Thomas Cloverdale had given Sam a Gospel tract . . .

* * *

On Friday, four days after having met the pastor, Sam parked the borrowed old, small pickup truck that had once been white but was now a dirty brown. Turning the engine off, he grabbed his doctor's bag, got out of the vehicle, and automatically reached out to close the door. He frowned when he remembered that the truck's doors had been removed, and then, shaking his head, he turned toward the building he'd parked in front of.

It was a one-story building that had been painted a bright, cheerful shade of yellow, but beneath the paint, Sam could clearly see that it was an old building. Although it had been well taken care of, he had the distinct impression that all it would take to bring it down was a strong gust of wind. Up above the wooden double doors, a large, white sign had been placed and the black letters on it declared that this was God's Children School. Sam figured, and rightly so, that one of the adjacent buildings was the actual orphanage.

As soon as Sam took a step away from the truck, he noticed a young woman wearing a bright green, short-sleeved cotton shirt that buttoned up the front; a bright green, loose-fitting skirt that swirled around her calves; and brown, gladiator-style sandals on her otherwise bare feet. She was seated on the topmost of the three concrete steps, but when he was halfway between the pickup and the school's entrance, he saw her stand up and walk toward him, a huge smile upon her face.

"You're the doctor, right? Dad says to tell you he's sorry but he couldn't meet you today because he's very busy, so he sent me instead," the woman said. As soon as she reached him, she stuck her hand out. "We really are grateful that you've come; all the kids have needed checkups, and you're an answer to prayer. I'm Esther Cloverdale, by the way. I teach here for both regular school and Sunday school. I love teaching kids and—"

"I'm sorry to interrupt, but I'd really like to get started examining the children, since it will probably take quite a while, depending on how many you have here," Sam said, shaking her hand even as he hoped the woman wouldn't be offended at being interrupted.

"Oh, dear, I'm sorry! Dad's always telling me that I ramble too much, but for some reason, I can't seem to keep quiet. What's your name? Dad told me, but I don't remember what it was. I'm terrible with names, so it might take me quite some time to remember yours."

"I'm Dr. Sam Gray," he answered as she moved to open one of the double doors.

"Is that short for Samuel? I've always thought that Samuel was such a nice name."

"No, it's just Sam."

"Well, Sam is a nice name, too, so don't feel bad. You look like a Sam, you know."

"You don't look like an Esther," Sam observed and heard her laugh at the words.

"I'll take that as a compliment. Don't get me wrong—I like my name—but Esther sounds so formal. So, did your wife come with you, or did she have to stay behind?"

"I'm not married," Sam answered.

"Really? That's good to know."

"What about you?" Sam asked, knowing she was waiting for him to ask her.

"Me? No, not yet. But I'm praying about it," Esther said readily, before rambling on about a new subject.

Sam smiled at her, even though she didn't see. Ordinarily, he would've found her talkative nature annoying, but he appreciated her easygoing manner and her ability to take everything he said in stride instead of getting offended at the least little thing like most people did nowadays. He didn't even find it all that annoying when she quoted several Bible verses at him.

It took two-and-a-half hours to perform checkups on all the children, and although at the end he was covered in sweat from the

African heat and his legs were aching, he was glad he'd come, for there were more than a handful of children who needed immediate medical treatment, most of them in the fourth grade class. Their conditions weren't serious yet, but Sam knew that would've changed in several weeks' time had he not come when he did.

"Well that's the last of them," Esther said happily as she walked Sam to the doors and out into the sunshine.

"I'll need to come back this Monday to treat the sick ones. Next time, I'll want to begin with the fourth grade children. There are a couple of children in that class whose conditions, if not treated as quickly as possible, could begin to rapidly deteriorate. I'll call your father this afternoon and let him know."

"Good, that means I won't need to remember to do it. It was nice meeting you, Sam, and thanks again for what you're doing for the kids," she said to him.

"I'm glad to help them, and it was nice meeting you, too. I'll see you Monday," Sam said as he left her standing in front of the steps while he went to the truck and climbed in.

"I'm looking forward to it!" she called out to him and waved cheerfully.

Sam grinned at her, started the old pickup's engine, and put the vehicle in reverse before putting it into drive. He waved back as he drove away and found that he, too, was looking forward to his return.

* * *

When Sam returned the following Monday morning, he had Laura Broderick, one of the nurses, with him. When he noticed that no one was waiting for him at the entrance, he went ahead and entered the school, then walked to the end of the hallway where he knew the fourth grade classroom was, the nurse following him. As Esther had done the last time he'd been here, Sam knocked upon the classroom door and waited; but after a few minutes went by and no one answered, he knocked again—a little harder this time. When the door opened, he found himself staring at Esther and was about to greet her when he felt a shock go through him, rendering him speechless.

She was five-feet-six-inches tall with waist-length hair the color of sun-kissed, ripened wheat, which had been parted in the middle and left to flow freely down her back, a round-shaped face, small button nose, and full, pink lips, her skin only lightly tanned despite having been in Africa for four years. She wore a pastel pink, short-sleeved dress that buttoned all the way up the front and came down almost to her ankles, hiding any curves she had, although it did nothing to hide her slender waist, her brown gladiator-style sandals once more on her feet. It was her eyes, however, that had taken Sam's ability to speak. Framed by long, thick eyelashes the same color as her hair were the most beautiful eyes Sam had ever seen in his entire life, the shade of them reminding him of the blue-green Caribbean waters in all those travel brochures advertising cruises.

How on earth did I ever miss those eyes?! he wondered as he stood before her, unable to speak or look away. He watched as her gaze went from him to the nurse beside him and then felt another shock surge through him when she turned her gaze back to him.

"Come in, Dr. Gray, but please be quiet until we're done with our current subject," she said, her voice all business.

Sam shook his head to clear it and then gave her a big smile. "Please, call me Sam," he told her as he followed her into the room.

"And if it's all the same to you, I'd rather treat the children now." He saw her pause and turn to look back at him, and once again, he found it difficult to look away from those Caribbean eyes.

"'But when Jesus heard that, he said unto them, They that be whole need not a physician, but they that are sick,' Matthew 9:12," one of the boys spoke up in accented English.

Esther smiled brightly. "Very good, Mshindi." Then, turning back to the doctor, she said, "I realize how important medical care is, *Dr. Gray,* but it can wait while I finish up with their current lesson."

"Don't take this the wrong way, but I think I liked you better outside your classroom," Sam said and grinned when the children began to snicker.

"I beg your pardon?" she said incredulously, her eyebrows rising.

"You're so serious today, it's a wonder you can get your students to pay attention to what you say." He felt an unpleasant chill when he saw those beautiful eyes suddenly narrow, clearly annoyed at his words.

"I assure you, Dr. Gray, the only one not paying attention to what I say is you," she said in a firm tone of voice, eliciting another round of snickers from the children. "Now if you'd be so kind as to take a seat and wait until we're finished . . . "

"Seriously, I liked you a lot better when you were being energetic and talkative, like you were on Friday," Sam remarked, which caused the students to outright laugh this time.

"On Friday? I have no idea what . . . " She gave a sigh then and changed what she was about to say. "She didn't tell you, did she. She never remembers to tell people, and this always happens. You'd think I'd be used to it by now."

"I don't know what you mean," Sam said, frowning in confusion.

"Sam, you *are* here!" exclaimed a merry voice from behind him.

Sam turned around and did a double-take when he saw the spitting image of the woman he'd just been conversing with, only this one was standing framed in the classroom doorway, a huge grin upon her face. Upon closer inspection, he realized that there were some differences.

The newcomer looked almost identical to the first woman, but instead of wearing a light pink dress that buttoned up the front, she wore a short-sleeved, sunflower yellow dress that zipped up in the back. Another difference between them was that while the first woman seemed to exude calm, having a steadiness clear for all to see, the newcomer was practically bouncing with excitement, her energy palpable. The most notable difference was that while the first woman had those incredible Caribbean eyes, the newcomer had hazel eyes, a warm brown with green flecks in them.

That's why I missed those eyes the first time, he realized. *They're two different people.*

"Esther, you didn't tell him," the first woman chastised the newcomer, although her tone was gentle and loving.

"Sorry, I forgot," Esther said.

"Twins," Sam said aloud, finally realizing the truth. "But if she's Esther, who are you?"

"'But by the grace of God I am what I am: and his grace which was bestowed upon me was not in vain; but I laboured more abundantly than they all: yet not I, but the grace of God which was with me,'" Esther quoted, laughing with amusement.

"First Corinthians 15:10," one of the girls said helpfully.

Sam watched as an amazing change came over the unidentified woman as she looked at the student who'd spoken up. Her features softened; her eyes began to sparkle wildly; and a slow smile crept over her face, revealing two dimples, one at each corner of her mouth.

"That's correct, Adisa. Well done," she praised the girl, and her smile widened when the girl's face beamed with pride.

"I'm afraid I don't understand," Sam said and once more saw those clear, blue-green eyes look his way.

"My name is Grace Cloverdale. Now, if you would please sit down at one of the empty desks so that I may finish the lesson, Dr. Gray, I would greatly appreciate it."

"Grace," he said softly and saw her raise a disapproving brow. "That's a pretty name. It suits you."

"That's what *I* always tell her, Sam," Esther chimed in, grinning as she walked into the room.

Sam forced himself to tear his gaze from Grace's eyes long enough to give Esther a friendly smile. "Nice to see you again, Esther."

"Glad you could make it, Sam," she said, grinning back at him.

Grace looked from the doctor to her sister. "Esther, remember what Dad has told you about doing that," she said.

Sam watched as Esther's grin faded to be replaced by a contrite expression, and he could just imagine how it felt to be on the receiving end of that soft, admonishing voice.

"I know, Grace, but it's *so difficult* sometimes," Esther said, her tone apologetic beneath her sister's loving reproof. "I'll try harder, I promise."

"'There hath no temptation taken you but such as is common to man: but God is faithful, who will not suffer you to be tempted above that ye are able; but will with the temptation also make a way to escape, that ye may be able to bear it,'" Grace quoted softly to her sister. Then, with that same gentle, disapproving stare, she looked at the doctor. "While I appreciate the compliment about my name, Dr. Gray, I would prefer that you call me and my sister 'Miss Cloverdale' when you address us."

Sam's heart nearly crumbled beneath that look, and he realized why Esther had been so quick to promise to try harder. The intense look combined with that tender soprano voice could've compelled even the hardest criminal to turn from his ways, Sam thought. He felt compelled to agree with her, but there was one problem with that. "How will you be able to tell which Miss Cloverdale I'm talking to when you're both in the room?" he asked her, thinking he'd trapped her. Another shock went through him when he saw her smile as though she'd somehow anticipated his question.

"Why, that's quite simple really. It will be the Miss Cloverdale at whom you are looking," Grace said matter-of-factly. Then, turning her attention back to her class, she said, "Class, let's resume today's Bible lesson now. What's the First Commandment?"

"'Thou shalt have no other gods before me,'" the children recited together.

"Second?"

"'Thou shalt not make unto thee any graven image.'"

"Third?"

"'Thou shalt not take the name of the Lord thy God in vain.'"

Sam sat in the back of the classroom and waited as the children recited all Ten Commandments and then individually answered questions about the Commandments, his eyes on Grace as she moved quietly around the room as though she was gliding instead of walking. When the bright sunshine streamed in through the window and caused her golden brown hair to shimmer, Sam found it difficult to breathe. When she was finally finished with the Bible lesson, it took three attempts and the children's laughter to gain his attention. As he moved to treat the worst of the children first, a single thought ran through his mind: *Why, oh, why did she have to be a missionary's daughter?*

* * *

"Good evening, Grace. How was your day?" Thomas Cloverdale asked later that night as Grace walked through the front door of their shared house.

"Uneventful for the most part, Dad," Grace answered. "What about yours?"

"Busy, but then when do I have a day that isn't?" he answered good-naturedly, giving his daughter a smile. "I hear you were mistaken for your sister again today."

"Esther must've beaten me home, I take it," said Grace, giving a longsuffering sigh.

"Yes, and we had a nice chat about her entire day, the highlight of which was you meeting Dr. Gray. Tell me, what did you think of him?"

Grace thought back to the six-foot-tall doctor with the dark brown hair and easy smile that lit up his laughing brown eyes the color of milk chocolate. She remembered his round-shaped face; strong, squared jawline; long, angular nose; medium tan skin; and rich and warm baritone voice. "He seems nice," she answered noncommittally, opening the coat closet door and pulling off her sandals to store them inside on the right, absently noting her sister's all the way on the left side. "I wish he wouldn't go from one extreme to another, though. It's unnerving."

Thomas frowned. "I'm not sure I follow your meaning, Grace."

"Well, I kept asking him to sit down so I could finish my Bible class with the kids, and he just kept saying how I needed to act more like the person he'd met Friday. This was before he realized I wasn't Esther, mind you; but still, he should've at least been courteous and sat down quietly until class was done. And then when he saw both Esther and me in the same room together, it was like he couldn't stop staring at me."

"Staring? Staring how?" the father pressed, wondering if he should be there the next time the doctor came to the school.

"It wasn't like that, Dad," Grace said calmly. "And once he did sit down at one of the desks in the back, his milk chocolate eyes followed me wherever I went inside the room."

Thomas raised a brow at his daughter's description of the young doctor's eyes, but he remained silent. He saw movement out of the corner of his eye and spied Esther coming in, her eyes shining mischievously as her mouth opened, and he knew she'd heard her sister's words. Catching Esther's eye, he surreptitiously shook his head *no* and saw her happy expression fall into disappointment.

Oblivious to the exchange, Grace then began to pace the empty area beside the couch, a frown on her face as her thoughts turned over. "And then when I was finally done with Bible and I told him he could proceed with his treatments, it was like he didn't even hear me, although he was staring right at me and could clearly see that I was speaking to him. I had to call him three times before I finally got him to pay attention. He'd been chomping at the bit to treat the kids when he'd gotten there, but when I finally told him he could, he just sat there like a knot on a log staring at me."

"Perhaps he was tuning out your Bible lesson," Thomas said.

"He didn't have that vacant, disinterested look that most get when they do that. It was . . . something else."

"What do you think it was?" he asked.

"I don't know, Dad," Grace said.

Esther grinned again and made her way into the living room. "Gracie and Dr. Sam sittin' in a tree, k-i-s-s-i-n-g! First comes love, then comes marriage, then comes—"

"Really, Esther, you're twenty-three years old," Grace chastised. "The least you could do is act like it."

"Grace, tell us more about those 'milk chocolate eyes' of his," Esther teased, though not maliciously.

Grace realized then what she'd said and felt her face grow hot with embarrassment. "It was a description, nothing more," Grace said defensively.

"Uh-huh," Esther said, unbelieving. "So what do you like most about him, sis?"

Grace put a palm over her face and sighed heavily, unwilling to give her sister any more ammunition to use against her.

"I like his smile," Esther said wistfully then. "He has a nice, friendly smile."

"I appreciate how much he seems to care about the children," Thomas said, hoping to prompt Grace to answer her sister's question. "What about you, Grace?"

"I'm going to go start supper now," Grace said, ignoring the question.

"Come on, Grace, answer the question!" Esther begged curiously.

"I just met him today; I don't even know him," Grace returned.

"From what little you do know of him, what do you like best?" Esther pressed her sister.

Grace didn't even have to think about her answer. "'His eyes are as the eyes of doves by the rivers of waters, washed with milk, and fitly set.'" She quoted Song of Solomon 5:12, her voice softening of its own accord. Then she turned and walked toward the kitchen, seeing in her mind the doctor's brown eyes staring back at her in shock as he had when she'd opened her classroom door to find him standing on the other side.

That night before she went to bed, Grace Cloverdale opened her well-worn Bible, took out her prayer list and an ink pen, and added Dr. Sam Gray's name to it under the "Unsaved" heading. Once done with that, Grace began to pray the kind-hearted doctor would be saved.

* * *

As Grace began her evening prayers, Sam was just climbing into bed, ready for a good night's rest after the long day he'd had. It was not to be, however, for just as soon as he closed his eyes, Grace's face appeared in his mind as it had looked that morning when she'd stood in the doorway of her classroom. Those beautiful eyes of hers had seemed to bore holes into his very being, and in her soft and gentle way of admonishment, she spoke earnestly to him about just one thing, repeating over and over again as though she waited for him to answer. *"If you died today, do you know where you would spend eternity? If you died today, do you know where you would spend eternity? If you died today, do you know . . ."*

CHAPTER TWO

"According to the grace of God which is given unto me, as a wise masterbuilder, I have laid the foundation, and another builded thereon. But let every man take heed how he buildeth thereupon."
1 Corinthians 3:10

ON SATURDAY, SAM WAS AT the open market, and from the looks of it, all of Africa was, too. He was looking at the little market stalls lined up on both sides of the crowded dirt road trying to decide what he needed the most, when he saw long, wheat-colored hair shining brightly in the afternoon sun. A smile lit up his face when he noted the bright red, short-sleeved blouse; the turquoise, tea-length skirt; and those unmistakable, gladiator-style, brown sandals. He knew it was Esther, for Grace always wore soft colors, while Esther always wore bright, vibrant colors. When he'd gone to the school the day before, Sam had been disappointed that Esther hadn't been able to accompany him as she normally did, for she'd needed to give her class a test, and so Sam was happy to find her here in the market. A grin broke out across his face as an amusing thought came to mind, and he walked up behind Esther, put his arms around her, and covered her eyes with his hands. "Guess who!" he said in English, laughing.

"Dr. Gray, kindly remove your hands from my person."

Sam immediately pulled his hands away, his laughter dying, for as soon as he heard that calm, quiet tone, he knew it wasn't Esther. His face burned with embarrassment, and when she turned to face him, those lovely Caribbean eyes gazing up at him with such patient disapproval, he felt that he'd committed the gravest of sins. "Grace! I'm so sorry; I thought you were—"

"I know very well who you thought I was," Grace said calmly.

"You're wearing bright colors, and you never wear bright colors," Sam explained nervously, inwardly frowning at himself for being embarrassed and nervous beneath her gaze.

"Yes, well, my sister decided to do laundry today; and in her haste to help, she gathered *all* of my clothes, dirty and otherwise, to wash. I had no choice but to borrow some of hers."

Sam chuckled as he pictured Esther doing that. "Does she do that often?"

Grace frowned. "No, not often. Only when she isn't thinking clearly about the task she's doing. Cooking is worse, though, so I'm the one who takes care of that chore. Otherwise, we'd be forced to eat burned food every night." Grace felt an odd warmth come over her when she heard his hearty laughter in her ears. It was the first time she'd heard him laugh, and she decided she liked it.

"Somehow, that doesn't surprise me at all. Well, I'm glad that she decided to wash all of your clothes. You look pretty in bright colors, Grace. You should wear them more often." He smiled gently at her and watched as her cheeks turned a pretty shade of light pink.

"Thank you, Dr. Gray, but please call me Miss Cloverdale. Also, you should not be so familiar with my sister or me, covering our eyes with your hands and things like that."

"Why? It was harmless, and it was supposed to be funny. Esther would've—"

"It doesn't matter what Esther would've done, Dr. Gray," Grace said quietly, that infinite patience in her eyes. "My sister and I are teachers in our father's school and part of the staff of his church. We have to think of our Christian testimony, and we don't want anyone to get the wrong idea about what kind of relationship we have with you. First Thessalonians 5:22 says, 'Abstain from all appearance of evil.' That means that not only should we as Christians try to refrain from sinning, but we should also refrain from even just the *appearance* of sin. You coming up to me and putting your hands on me may seem innocent enough to you, but most everyone knows I'm a missionary's daughter and it would make them think that my relationship with you is more than what it is. Do you understand what I'm trying to say?"

"Sort of," Sam answered, now feeling thoroughly ashamed of his actions. Oh, he knew she wasn't trying to be mean or make him feel bad about what he'd done, for he couldn't imagine Grace having a mean bone in her entire body; but that gentle tone and the patient, disapproving look in her eyes just made him want to do whatever it took to get her to look at him just once with respect and approval. "Why do you do that anyway?"

Grace blinked, uncomprehending, and asked, "Do what exactly?"

"Quote Bible verses all the time. And it isn't just you. Your dad and sister do it, too. Why is that?"

"It's the best way to remember the verses," she answered and gave him a soft smile.

Sam felt his heart being squeezed at her smile. "Why do you need to remember them, though? I mean, isn't that why you have

Bibles?" For the first time since he'd met her, Sam heard Grace laugh. It was lighthearted, musical, and caused her eyes to shine so beautifully that Sam had a difficult time holding her gaze. Somehow, he knew she wasn't laughing at him, for he could still see that gentle understanding that he'd only seen in her.

"There are two reasons why we have the Bible. First is because the Bible says, 'Study to shew thyself approved unto God, a workman that needeth not to be ashamed, rightly dividing the word of truth.' That's in 2 Timothy 2:15. We may read a verse one day and get a specific lesson from it but then read the same verse two days later and get a completely different lesson from it. As we read the Bible, God speaks to our hearts and gives us whatever truth He knows we need at the time. The second reason is because Jesus commanded all Christians to 'go ye therefore, and teach all nations, baptizing them in the name of the Father, and of the Son, and of the Holy Ghost: Teaching them to observe all things whatsoever I have commanded you,' which is found in Matthew 28:19-20."

"But you teach them in class. You don't need to memorize verses to do that. You have your Bible right there on your desk; I have seen it."

"All right, then, let's say I come to the market, and I'm here to get food. I know I will need quite a bit, which means I can't carry my Bible with me. Well, I meet someone who isn't saved, and I feel the Holy Spirit telling me that I need to speak to this person. How am I to go down the Roman's Road with him if I haven't memorized it and I didn't bring my Bible with me?"

"The . . . the what?" he asked.

Grace smiled at him, having hoped that he would ask. Silently, she began to pray for Dr. Gray's soul and for the Holy Spirit to convict the doctor of his need for salvation. Aloud, she answered, "The Roman's Road. They are verses found in the book of Romans."

"I . . . I guess you wouldn't be able to if you didn't have your Bible and you hadn't memorized the verses," Sam said.

"Exactly," she responded, nodding. "But because I have memorized them, I could explain that Romans 3:10 says, 'As it is written, There is none righteous, no, not one,' which means you, me, my sister, my father—none of us are good. Then I can quote Romans 3:23, which says, 'For all have sinned, and come short of the glory of God.' From there, I can tell the person that even though we may do good things, we're still all sinners by God's standard. Then I can explain *how* we all became sinners by quoting Romans 5:12, which says 'Wherefore, as by one man sin entered into the world, and death by sin; and so death passed upon all men, for that all have sinned.' That one man was Adam. Then it gets to the price of our sins in Romans 6:23. The first part says, 'For the wages of sin is death.' Well, you're a smart man, Dr. Gray. You know what wages are, right?"

"Wages are something you earn. Like money is my wage for my work as a doctor."

"Just so, but you'd be surprised how many people I talk to who don't know. Okay, so just like you earn wages for your job, everyone also earns a wage for our sin and, as it says in that verse, the wages of *sin* is death. So the previous verses have said that there is none righteous, and all have sinned; that we sin because Adam sinned, which brought sin into the world; with sin, he brought death in also; and because all of us have sinned, all of us must face death as punishment."

As she spoke, Sam couldn't help but notice how her expression was the same as when she was in class teaching her young students something. But as he watched her, the words echoing in his mind, he saw a brilliant smile light up her expression, brighten her eyes, and put a pretty blush into her cheeks.

"Now we come to the good part. I told you that the first part of Romans 6:23 was, 'For the wages of sin is death.' But that isn't the whole verse, and it's the second part that explains how you can escape paying for your sins with your death. 'For the wages of sin is death; but the gift of God is eternal life through Jesus Christ our Lord.' So, we owe a sin debt, and that sin debt is our life, but God gave us the gift of eternal life because He doesn't want us to die in our sins. And Romans 5:8 tells us *why* He doesn't want us to die in our sins and what He did to keep us from it. 'But God commendeth his love toward us, in that, while we were yet sinners, Christ died for us.' Imagine it, Dr. Gray! We lie, steal, murder, ignore God, deny His existence, and do all kinds of other evil things, and *still* He loves us enough to send His Son Jesus to die for us! Another amazing thing is that God didn't make it difficult for us to get His gift. He knows we aren't perfect and that we can never be perfect, so we can't work our way into Heaven. There's only one way we can get to Heaven, and that is through Jesus. God explains to us in Romans 10:13 that 'whosoever shall call upon the name of the Lord shall be saved.' Romans 10:9 says, 'That if thou shalt confess with thy mouth the Lord Jesus, and shalt believe in thine heart that God hath raised him from the dead, thou shalt be saved.' So I explain to this person that I've run into at the market that you must believe that Jesus is God's Son; that He lived a sinless life, died on the cross, and was raised again on the third day. Then I explain to him that to receive eternal life from God, he merely needs to pray and ask God to forgive him for all of his sins and for Jesus to come into his heart and save him. Now, just think how difficult that would be for me to tell him all of that if I hadn't memorized all of those verses!"

Sam had never seen calm, collected Grace Cloverdale as animated and enthusiastic as she was as she spoke of this so-called Roman's Road. Her bright, shining eyes seemed to dance, her whole face practically glowed, her cheeks were flushed with excitement, and Sam couldn't remember having ever seen her look as beautiful as she did right then. Not once did he ever guess that it was to *him* she'd been witnessing. "I can see how that would be difficult to do," he said, staring into her eyes.

"That reminds me," Grace said suddenly. "I've been meaning to invite you to church, but you're always so busy with the children that I didn't want to interrupt. Would you come tomorrow?" Once more, Grace began to pray fervently, hoping he would say yes and not just because she wanted to see him again. She knew he wasn't saved—she could feel it—and she wanted more than anything else in the world to see him come to accept Jesus as his Savior.

Sam saw the hope burning in her eyes and felt uncomfortable beneath her frank, open gaze. "I can't; I have to work," he said and felt guilty when he saw her hopeful expression fade. He was telling the truth, but he knew that if he hadn't had to work, he would've found a way to tell her no.

"On a Sunday?" she questioned, trying not to show how disappointed she was.

"I'm afraid so," he answered. "Usually we don't, but there are so many people here in desperate need of medical care that the powers that be decided to keep the medical tent open on Sundays to help with it, at least for now."

"How long will you have to work?" she asked. "Maybe you can make it to the evening service."

"It depends on how busy I'll be, so I won't really know until tomorrow."

"Can you ask off then?" she questioned him.

Sam could still see a glimmer of hope in her eyes, and he hated to kill it, but he knew she'd prefer the truth. "It's too close to Sunday for me to do that now," he answered and saw that last glimmer finally die.

"What about next Sunday then?"

"We'll see," Sam said to her.

Grace knew by the tone of his voice that he didn't want to agree, whether he was working or not; so with wisdom, she decided to not press him on the subject and just continue to pray, knowing that God would continue to work on his heart. "So how are the kids doing, Dr. Gray?" she asked him and saw him instantly relax at the change of subject.

"Much better than when I first examined them. They are responding well to the treatments, showing no adverse effects, and I'm very pleased about it," Sam said and saw her smile at the good news.

"I'm glad of that. You don't know how long everyone at the church has been praying for this. We're all so grateful to you for what you're doing for the children."

"I'm happy to be helping the kids," Sam said. "Oh, by the way, I've been meaning to ask you something."

Grace bit her lip and turned to the market stand they were standing in front of, feeling her heart beating rapidly and trepidation in her soul, for the thought that he was about to ask her out suddenly entered her head. Switching to Swahili to address the stall worker, she asked him for some of the oats he was selling, gathering up her courage and calming her heart down. "What is it that you want to ask me, Dr. Gray?" she asked him, switching back to English, and her voice came out as calm as it always was, despite how she was feeling inside.

"I've been meaning to ask you for your phone number." He saw her stiffen immediately, which caused him to frown.

"My phone number?" she asked, unable to keep the surprise from her voice.

"Yes," Sam said, amused at hearing the surprise in her tone. "That way, if I need to discuss one of your students without them hearing, I'll be able to simply call you and discuss the matter." He watched her look at him, saw her eyes searching his, and felt that she could see that he wasn't just asking for her number to talk to her about her students, which was why her response shocked him so much.

"That would be a good idea, wouldn't it," she remarked and then shifted the bag of oats to reach into a skirt pocket to pull something out. "Here you go. Feel free to call me whenever you need. If no one's there, the machine will answer it, so just leave a message."

I can't believe it! She actually gave me her number! Sam thought excitedly to himself. "I will, thank you."

"You're welcome. Now, if you'll excuse me, I must get home. I've got to prepare my Sunday school lesson for tomorrow morning. It was nice talking to you, Dr. Gray."

"Please, call me Sam," he implored her.

Grace smiled at his exasperated tone and said, "Have a good day, Dr. Gray," before she walked away from him.

Sighing in defeat, he remembered that she'd given him her phone number, and the thought caused his mood to lighten again. Grinning like a fool, he looked at the piece of paper in his hand and felt annoyance bubbling up inside him. He looked back up to see her walking away, the sea of dark faces parting for her politely whenever they could. *You're just as sneaky as your father, Grace Cloverdale,* he thought. As he stared back down at the Gospel tract she'd given to him—one identical to the one given to him by her father on the day Sam had met Dr. Cloverdale—one phrase from their conversation came back to him, and he could hear her voice in his mind just as clearly as if she was still standing in front of him repeating it to him.

"For the wages of sin is death; for the wages of sin is death; for the wages of sin is . . ."

* * *

As soon as Grace got home that evening, Thomas immediately noticed that something was bothering her. Before he could ask her what was wrong, Esther, who was busy folding clothes from the clean pile on the couch, spoke up.

"Grace, did you get the oats?" Esther asked, pausing in her whistling to speak.

"Right here," Grace said, holding up the sack she carried, her mind reviewing the conversation she'd had with Sam—*Dr. Gray,* she reminded herself, gritting her teeth.

"And the sugar?" Esther prompted and watched as her sister flinched.

"Oh, I don't believe it!" Grace moaned, shaking her head deprecatingly. "I completely forgot about the sugar!"

Esther walked over to Grace and placed a palm on her sister's forehead. "You must be sick or something. You never forget *anything*."

"That isn't funny, Esther," Grace said.

"Seriously, Grace, what's the matter? This isn't like you, and you look preoccupied with something," Esther said, frowning at her sister.

Once again, Grace didn't think before she answered. "'It was but a little that I passed from them, but I found him whom my soul loveth.'" She quoted from Song of Solomon 3:4 and her voice was quiet, her eyes full of unhappiness. She turned away and went into the kitchen to put up the bag of oats and then walked back into the living room, heading for the door. "I'll be back with the sugar in a little while, Esther," she said with resignation and then left the house without another word.

Esther looked at her father and said, "Dad, she's quoting Song of Solomon again. What's going on with her?"

"Pray for her, Esther," Thomas said, worry on his face. "She's going to be needing it now more than ever."

Esther just shrugged and went back to folding the clean clothes, confusion plain on her face.

That evening, Grace had her Bible opened on her bed, her prayer list in her hand as she prayed for those on it, and tried desperately to not see Sam Gray's face in her mind.

* * *

"Please, *please* let me sleep tonight," Sam said aloud to no one as he lay down in the bed, for since he'd met Grace, he'd been unable to sleep. As soon as he turned the light out, the litany inside his mind began once again, unsettling him as he heard her pretty voice calmly repeating; but this time, it was different and so much worse than before, those soft-spoken words and gentle, sad eyes wounding his heart.

"For the wages of sin is death. If you died today, do you know where you would spend eternity? For the wages of sin is death. If you died today, do you know where you would spend eternity? For the wages of sin is death . . . "

CHAPTER THREE

*"That the name of our Lord Jesus Christ may be glorified in you, and ye
in him, according to the grace of our God and the Lord Jesus Christ."*

2 Thessalonians 1:12

TWO WEEKS AFTER THE RUN-IN at the market, Sam pulled up in
front of the school building, parked the truck and got out, looking
forward to once again seeing Grace. After the meeting in the market,
she'd been kind of standoffish with him, although never unkind,
and Sam couldn't figure out why she was acting so strangely. *Well,
stranger than she usually did,* he amended the thought as he began to
walk toward the double doors. He frowned when he saw Grace seated
on the steps wearing a dismally gray dress and black sandals, her face
lowered so that he couldn't see it. She had not looked up at the sound
of his truck, nor did she seem to notice his approach.

"Grace?" he called to her, but when she reacted to the name, he
saw it was Esther instead and that her hazel eyes were red and puffy.
"Esther, what's the matter?" he asked and saw her rise to her feet.

"Both Dad and I tried to call you, but neither of us could get ahold
of anyone until after you'd already left." Esther wiped a tear away.

Sam knew whatever had happened had to have been serious to make
an optimistic, sunny person like Esther cry. "Esther, what's wrong?"

"You'll have to come back another time. The school is closed today. If you call Dad later, you'll be able to schedule when you can come back."

"I can just go to the orphanage and check the kids out there today since school is closed," Sam said, knowing that Esther would not explain herself until she got through the necessary stuff, for it was her habit to do so since she had trouble remembering things.

"No, not today, Sam. Today isn't a good day for the kids."

"That's fine, Esther," Sam said, a small smile on his lips every time she spoke his name, for unlike her sister, Esther had never been able to refer to him as *Dr. Gray*. "If I can just give Mshindi his medicine, I'll be on my way."

Esther wiped another tear. "I'm sorry, Sam, but you can't."

"Esther, Mshindi needs his medicine. If he doesn't get his weekly shot, he could relapse back into his illness again before he's fully healed. The other students can wait, but—"

"You don't understand, Sam," Esther said as tears rolled down her cheeks. "Mshindi doesn't need his shots anymore. He went Home early this morning."

"Home?" Sam repeated, confused. "The orphanage is his home. Esther, what is wrong? Why are you crying?"

"I mean he went Home to Heaven, Sam," Esther clarified and wiped some more tears away.

"He . . . he's *dead*?!" For what seemed like forever, Sam could only stare in astonished silence as his brain tried to process the thought that the child he'd been caring for was dead. He felt like someone had thrown a bucket of freezing cold water on his head. When he finally found his voice, he said, "I don't understand. He was fine when I saw him last. What happened?"

"I don't know all the details, but I do know it was a snake bite. We've closed the school, and—"

"Oh, no. *Grace!*" he exclaimed, knowing how much Grace loved each of her students. Sam looked at Esther, his only thoughts now of how Grace was handling it. "Esther, do you know where she is?"

"Yes," Esther answered. "She's in her classroom alone. But she won't want anyone to—"

"Laura, stay here with Esther," Sam told the nurse and then flung open the door to the school, running toward the classroom at the end of the hallway. He knocked several times on the door but when no one answered, he quietly opened it and looked in.

Dressed in a bright yellow blouse, matching skirt, and white sandals, Grace was seated at Mshindi's school desk, her eyes looking toward the front of the class as though paying attention to a teacher only she could see and hear. Her face showed no expression; and unlike her sister, her eyes weren't red or puffy, and there were no tears rolling down her face.

Sam stepped into the room and quietly closed the door, then walked over to sit down at the desk in front of Mshindi's, turning around to face her, his eyes looking into hers. "Grace?" he called her name softly.

"How many times must I ask you, Dr. Gray, to please call me Miss Cloverdale?" she admonished him in that gentle way of hers.

Smiling at her, hoping to cheer her up, he answered, "As many times as I have to ask you to call me Sam." He saw her smile, but it wasn't like she was smiling to prove to him that she was okay even when she wasn't. This was a genuine smile, and it lit up her eyes just as all of her other smiles did. It made him wonder if she was in denial about the boy's death. "I heard about Mshindi. I'm so sorry, Grace."

She looked at him curiously and asked, "Sorry for what?"

"That he's gone. Are you okay?"

"Of course I am. Why wouldn't I be?" she responded, her voice full of sincere confusion.

Sam frowned because he, too, was confused. "Because he's dead." That's when he saw a huge smile come over her, one that caused her cheeks to flush and her face to glow.

"'We are confident, I say, and willing rather to be absent from the body, and to be present with the Lord.' Second Corinthians 5:8," she said. "I led him to the Lord about a month ago. I am happy that he's with the Lord now."

Sam's mouth dropped open at her words, his brown eyes wide with shock. "You—you're *happy* he's dead? How can you be so *cold* about the death of a child?!" She seemed to bristle at his last words, and he knew he was in for it as soon as he saw her meet his gaze. She did not start yelling or breaking down into tears like most women would've done. What she did was far worse, at least to Sam's thinking.

Sitting up straight in the desk, Grace seemed to draw strength from an unknown Source, and the inner peace she always seemed to have in abundance shone through her blue-green eyes as she studied the confused and shocked expression on Sam's face. "You think I'm being cold about his death? This morning at the beginning of the school day, he sat here just as he did every school day, his curious black eyes watching me as they always did. Bible was his favorite subject, and so he always loved that I started every school day off with teaching the Bible. Today was no different, at first. We got to the recitation of the

Ten Commandments. We were on the fifth commandment when I noticed him stand up without permission and begin to walk toward me. It wasn't usual behavior from him, but I was in the middle of the lesson; so instead of asking him what he was doing, I simply told him to sit back down. He didn't do it, and it surprised me; but I told him a second time to sit back down. I didn't think anything was wrong because I was looking at his face and he seemed so calm. It wasn't until Eidi screamed that I realized something was very wrong. But by then, it was too late. The snake had come in through a hole in the wall, and I hadn't seen it. My walking around must've agitated it because it came toward me first. Mshindi had seen it and knew it was venomous, but he didn't want to start a panic in the class, so he was going to walk over to me and quietly whisper it in my ear. He realized he didn't have enough time, and so instead, he put his foot in front of mine and took the strike that was meant for me."

Sam watched as a tear leaked out of one eye, but she didn't bother to wipe it away. He expected her voice to break over her next words, but her tone was still just as calm and strong as it ever was.

"One of the other boys had a knife, and while Mshindi held the snake with one foot, the other boy stabbed it to death. It took only seconds before he couldn't stand; and I knew there was nothing I could do, so I held him. Right over there, right in front of my desk, I held him in my arms as he died, Dr. Gray. It was an ugly, painful death, but he tried to keep the pain from his face and talked to me about how he couldn't wait to see Jesus and to see his mansion and walk upon the street of gold. When he began having seizures and could no longer speak, I held him tighter and quoted verse after verse from all the descriptions of what Heaven is like. When he bit his tongue off, I ordered all the other children outside because I didn't want them to see. He lost all control over his bodily functions before finally, mercifully, he went home to be with the Lord."

Sam watched her stand up and walk to her desk, open up a drawer, pull out a small stack of papers, and then walk back to him, handing the papers to him. Her eyes watching him expectantly, she stared at him as he looked down to see what was in his hand. When he read what was on the first page, he felt a deep sense of self-loathing come over him for his assumption.

"I received them just this morning before school. I never even got the chance to show them to him or tell him my request to formally adopt him had been granted. He was special to me; I loved him dearly, and I had to hold him and watch as his life seeped out of him in one of the cruelest ways imaginable. I am happy he's in Heaven, that he no longer must feel pain, that he no longer must experience hunger or worry about danger of any kind, and that he is finally, at long last, with his Heavenly Father. But at the same time, I am sad he had to die that way, sad that I did not get to tell him about the adoption papers being accepted, sad that I will never again see his sweet face seated at his desk, his eyes shining with excitement for the morning's Bible lesson, and sad that I will never be able to take him home with me and give him his own room. He gave his life to save me, Dr. Gray, and I'll never be able to repay that. If not for what he did this morning, it would be *me* lying in a box about to be buried this afternoon."

Only after she'd finished did she begin to weep softly; yet even then, Sam could see that strength and peace surrounding her. But he had none, for he kept picturing her dying instead of Mshindi; and it caused a mixture of horror, fear, and relief in him. Her soft-spoken words felt like daggers plunging into his heart, making him feel like the worst human being on the face of the earth for assuming that she didn't care about Mshindi's death. Regret and shame in his eyes, he stood up and gently took her by the shoulders, looking down into those eyes of hers.

"Grace, I'm so sorry," he whispered hoarsely. "I should never have believed that you could be apathetic toward anyone's death, much less a child's. Please, Grace, forgive me for saying that . . . for *thinking* that." Then, before she answered him, he pulled her against him and wrapped his arms around her.

* * *

Grace closed her eyes and breathed in his masculine scent and wished that she could cry out all of her sadness as he comforted her in his strong arms, but she knew it would be inappropriate. She did not wish him to think she was backing away due to not forgiving him, and so she answered his words first. "I know you don't see death the same way as I do," she told him quietly, "and I also know that it can be very confusing. I understand why you said what you said, and I'm not upset with you." Grace's eyes shut tighter when she felt his hand on the back of her head and when she felt him pull away from her just enough to look down into her eyes, she forced herself to meet his gaze. *Give me strength, Lord, please!* she prayed fervently.

"Does that mean you do forgive me?" he asked her and began to wipe away the tears from her face.

"I forgive you," she said and then stepped out of his arms and walked to her desk to sit behind it, hoping to keep a safe distance away from him, wanting to still be in his arms. She was acutely aware of it when he followed her to stand beside her desk, his eyes on her.

"Grace—"

"Miss Cloverdale," she corrected gently.

"*Grace,*" he began again, saying her first name firmly, "will you be all right?"

"'Blessed are they that mourn: for they shall be comforted,'" she quoted with a soft smile on her face. "That's Matthew 5:4," she added helpfully.

Sam put his hand over both of hers, which were folded together atop her desk, and looked down into her eyes when she looked up at him. "If there's anything I can do, Grace, let me know. Your dad has the phone number to the house where I'm staying."

"Thank you, Dr. Gray," she said.

"Sam," he corrected with a grin, knowing what she was going to say. He saw her lips twitch with amusement, and then she was laughing softly.

"*Dr. Gray,*" she said just as firmly as he'd said her name and heard him begin to chuckle.

"You're welcome, Grace. I'll see you next time." Sam was opening the door when he heard her call to him.

"Dr. Gray?"

"Yes?"

"Next time, please leave the door open. You and I shouldn't be alone together in a room with the door open, much less with it closed," she said.

Puzzled, Sam asked, "Why not?"

"'Abstain from all appearance of evil.' Remember?"

"I'll try to remember next time, Grace," he said and then left.

Grace watched him leave the room and then stood up, walking only as far as she needed to so that she could follow him down the hallway with her eyes. She knew that something had changed profoundly between them, knew that it would become increasingly harder to fight him, and so she prayed as she watched Sam leave the school, asking God once more to convict his heart of his need for salvation.

* * *

Twenty-four-year-old Dr. Tanya Jackson walked into the medical tent's makeshift breakroom, pushing her shoulder-length, black hair behind her ears, her toned stomach rumbling with hunger. She smiled when she noticed Sam seated at one of the small folding tables but frowned when she noticed the dark circles under his eyes and his weary face. "Sam, you okay?" she asked him.

"Yeah," Sam lied and winced when he pictured Grace's disapproving look and heard her voice saying, *Thou shalt not lie.* He groaned and ran both hands through his hair, for this had been happening every single day for the past week. Every time he broke one of the commandments, he could hear her recite it, and he was growing nervous about seeing her tomorrow, thinking that she might somehow know how much he'd sinned. To make matters worse, he was getting very little sleep at night, the litany echoing over and over inside his mind in her voice. He knew he needed to talk to someone about it, and he'd considered going to Grace, but something always held him back from doing so.

"Seriously, Sam, you look like you haven't slept in ages," Tanya said.

"I feel like I haven't," Sam said, exhaustion in his voice. "I'm having trouble sleeping at night."

Tanya went over to the sandwich vending machine that had been set up for the physicians and began digging in her slacks pocket for her change. Finding that she was a nickel short, she turned to Sam and asked him if he had a spare nickel he could give to her.

Sam dug into his pocket until he found one then held it out to her. "'Ask and ye shall receive,'" he said automatically and then frowned. "Great, now she's got *me* doing it," he muttered to himself.

Tanya didn't hear him mutter, so she continued with the conversation by asking him a question. "Girl trouble?" she teased him, trying to lighten his mood. His next words surprised her.

"How did you know?" Sam watched her turn around to face him, and he realized she'd only been teasing him. *Great, I gave it away*, he thought to himself unhappily.

"Wait, *really*? Who is she?"

Sam let his forehead fall onto the table as he shut his eyes, thinking maybe he was in a nightmare and that he'd wake up feeling refreshed and like himself again. "I don't really want to talk about it, Tanya."

Tanya got her food and then sat down across from Sam, her black eyes on the top of his head since she couldn't see his face. "No, you've gotta tell me who she is. You can't keep me in suspense!"

"Tell you who *who* is?" asked Laura, the nurse who'd been accompanying Sam to the God's Children School.

"Sam is having girl trouble," Tanya said, "but he won't tell me who this girl is."

"You mean you haven't heard yet?" Laura asked and saw Tanya frown as Sam scowled.

"You know who she is?"

"Of course I do. I thought everyone did. He likes Miss Cloverdale," Laura reported. She grinned when Sam moaned as though he was in pain.

"The *missionary's daughter*? You've got to be kidding me!" Tanya exclaimed. She frowned and asked, "Wait a minute, which Miss Cloverdale? The chatterbox or the other one?"

Sam's scowl returned to his face at hearing Esther being referred to as a chatterbox, but knowing she'd probably laugh if she heard it, he decided not to say anything about it.

"He likes Grace," Laura said as she put her coins in the drink machine.

Tanya's eyebrows rose up as high as they could, and she stared incredulously at Sam. "I can understand why you'd fall for the chatterbox. She's funny and talkative and has a fairly good sense of humor. But Grace Cloverdale? I swear, she acts like if she cracked a smile, her whole face would break apart! And she walks around here like she's better than everyone else!"

"She does not," Sam refuted and felt his face reddening in anger.

"Oh, yes she does! She acts like everyone else who doesn't buy into her stupid religion is beneath her, and it makes me sick just to look at her!"

"She does *not* act that way, Tanya," Sam repeated, his brown eyes darkening slightly with anger.

"I mean seriously, Sam, what could you possibly see in Little-Miss-Holier-Than-Thou—"

Both Tanya and Laura jumped as Sam brought a fist down forcefully upon the table at which he was sitting, rising swiftly to his feet as he glared at the black-haired woman. "Grace is a kind, humble, classy, and compassionate woman who cares about everyone whether they care about her or not, and I will not sit here and listen to you insult her!"

Tanya watched as Sam moved to leave and she caught his arm as he passed. "Sam, listen to me for a minute. You should forget about her. She won't want anything to do with you. If you try to pursue a relationship with her, you'll just get your heart broken. You realize that, right?"

"Grace would never hurt a fly," he said, pulling his arm loose from her before storming out of the room.

* * *

After a very long, busy day, Sam walked out of the medical tent, his stomach growling loudly, but he didn't want to go home to eat. Pondering where he could go to get a bite to eat, his thoughts were interrupted by a pair of African men dressed in business suits.

"Good afternoon," the older man said in Swahili, a pleasant smile on his face. "I was wondering if I could speak to you about something for a little while."

Sam looked at them skeptically and asked, "You're not selling anything, are you?"

"Oh, no, sir," the older man said. "What we have is a free gift. All you must do is to accept it."

"A free gift?" Sam repeated, his eyes narrowing with suspicion. "What's this free gift?"

"I'll get to that in a second, but first, do you mind if I ask you a question? It will take only a moment."

"Well, all right, but I've had a very long day today. I'd really like to get some food and go home," Sam said, hoping he wouldn't regret it.

"If you died today, do you know where you would spend eternity?"

Sam blinked two or three times, and then he glared at them. "Did Grace put you up to this?"

"Grace?" the older man repeated, confused.

"Yes, Grace Cloverdale. Did she put you up to this?"

"You know Sister Cloverdale?" the older man asked, surprised.

"She did put you up to this," Sam said, so certain of his words.

"Um, no, sir," the older man answered. "Pastor Cloverdale did, actually."

"He would've been my second guess. Well, you tell him that if he wants to know where I'd spend eternity, he can come ask me himself," Sam huffed out.

"I think there's been a misunderstanding," the older man said. "Pastor Cloverdale organizes the adults and teenagers of Lighthouse Baptist Church to go witnessing once a week every week, and today is the day we do that. He doesn't send us to any specific location or to any particular person, unless the person has requested a visit. We go where the Lord leads us to go, sir."

"Are you *sure* Grace didn't send you to talk to me?"

"I am quite positive, sir. Why? How do you know Sister Cloverdale?"

"I'm Dr. Sam Gray; I've been treating the children at the—"

"Why, Dr. Gray, it's a pleasure to finally meet you! We've heard so much about you!" the older man said, taking Sam's hand and shaking it enthusiastically.

"You . . . you have?"

"Yes, sir! Our church had been praying for so long for medical help for those children, and then the Lord sent you! Both Pastor and Sister Cloverdale speak very highly of you."

Sam continued to speak to them, barely noticing the old, gray minivan that came tearing around the corner and into the parking lot to come sliding to a stop. He didn't notice the person jump out of the van or slide the large door open, and he didn't notice the driver pull a young boy out of the back. What finally caught his attention was the shouting.

"Help! Someone help me, please!"

Sam immediately turned to the voice and gasped when he saw Grace running for the medical tent, one of her students held in her arms. Sam ran straight for her and when he reached her, he took the boy from her, recognizing him as Machupa. "Follow me and tell me what happened, Grace," he said to her, hurrying back inside the tent. Bypassing those who were waiting, he took Machupa straight back to the room he'd used all day and put him onto the cot.

"They were having recess, and about halfway through, he came over to me and complained that his stomach hurt. I told him he could go lie down at his desk if he wanted, and he did. But before he could get to the classroom, he doubled over in pain and started vomiting. I called in the rest of my class, put them in with Esther's, and drove as fast as I could over here. I didn't know what else to do."

Sam unbuttoned the boy's jeans and pulled his shirt up. "Why didn't you take him to the emergency room?" he asked.

"You were closer, and I figured if it wasn't serious, you could take care of it here."

Sam pressed down on the boy's stomach, and it didn't take much pressure to cause the boy to vomit, which only confirmed his suspicion. "We've got to get him to the hospital right now," he told Grace, his expression concerned.

"Dr. Gray, we don't have the money for—"

Sam grabbed Grace's shoulder and pulled her aside, lowering his voice so the boy wouldn't hear. "Listen to me; he's suffering from appendicitis and needs emergency surgery. If he doesn't get help soon, his appendix will rupture, and he'll die."

"Oh, dear God, *no!*" Grace cried out in alarm.

Sam went to the boy and picked him up in his arms, frowning at Grace's horrified reaction, which would've been anyone else's reaction, too, except Sam had never known Grace to react normally to any situation before.

"How long will it be? How soon can we get there? Will—"

"Grace," Sam said to her as he carried the boy to his truck, the worried schoolteacher following closely behind, "calm down. Don't forget, if anything happens, he'll go to Heaven, right? Remember your faith."

"I haven't lost my faith, Dr. Gray! You don't understand! Machupa isn't saved yet! If something happens to him, he won't go to Heaven! He'll go to Hell!"

* * *

Sam put the boy in the back of the truck and then turned to help Grace up.

Grace's eyes widened when she felt Sam's hands on her waist, and the next thing she knew, his strong arms were lifting her up and into the truck beside the boy. Her eyes darted to Sam and saw him rush to get into the truck, cranking the engine over.

"Hang on!" he called out and then threw the vehicle into gear before stepping on the accelerator.

"Miss Cloverdale?" the young boy said in Swahili as Grace tried to keep him as still as possible on the gutted-out truck floor.

"Yes?" she answered in the same manner.

"I . . . I don't wanna die and go to Hell."

Grace looked into the frightened boy's eyes and felt a sudden calm steal over her soul. "If you want, I can tell you how you can stay out of Hell. Would you like that?"

"Y . . . yes, ma'am."

As she had done with Sam at the marketplace, Grace led the young boy down the Roman's Road of salvation, making sure the boy understood exactly what he was doing and knowing full well that the man driving the truck was listening to every word that was being said.

Just before they reached the hospital, even though the boy was still in a lot of pain, Machupa closed his eyes and prayed for forgiveness, asking Jesus to come into his heart and save him.

When the boy had finished, Grace looked into the boy's eyes and smiled that big smile of hers. "Now, just think, you are no longer an orphan, for you have a Heavenly Father who will love you no matter what happens," she said to the boy.

"Miss Cloverdale, I need to get baptized now, don't I?"

Grace smiled at the boy's willingness to obey and answered. "God commands all new Christians to be baptized to show to everyone else what has already happened in your heart and also to prove to God that you're serious about wanting to follow Him and do what's right."

Sam pulled into the hospital's parking lot and found an empty parking place. Shutting off the engine, he jumped out of the truck and then climbed up into the back of the pickup. As Grace stood up, Sam grabbed her around the waist again and then gently lowered her down to the ground before picking up the boy and getting out of the truck.

"Will you *please* not do that again, Dr. Gray?" Grace admonished, turning her gaze away to keep him from seeing her blush at the unexpected contact.

"Not do what?" Sam asked, his mind on the child and not thinking of how Grace wouldn't approve of the familiar contact.

Grace realized that Sam had no idea what he'd done wrong, so focused on getting help for Machupa was he, so for once, she decided to let it go. "Never mind, Dr. Gray, don't worry about it."

"Miss Cloverdale, I really do need to get baptized now."

"My dear boy, we don't have deep water, and we don't have a pastor to baptize you. You'll need to wait."

"But what happens if I . . . if I die? Won't God be angry with me for not obeying?"

"God knows you're very sick, and He also knows where we are right now. He understands why you can't get baptized. He won't get angry with you. In fact, He's very pleased that you want to obey Him this much."

"I need to do it, Miss Cloverdale! I need to!"

"Sweetheart, I—"

"Sister Cloverdale, how are you?" a deep voice boomed across the parking lot.

Grace looked up and saw the assistant pastor of her church coming out of the hospital and over to where she was. "Brother Kweli,

Machupa has appendicitis, and he needs prayer. Can you call the church and have them begin a prayer chain for him, please?"

"Of course!" the African man answered readily.

"Brother Kweli, guess what!" the boy said, grinning.

"What?"

"I just got saved!"

"Why, that is *wonderful*! Welcome to God's family, my brother in Christ!"

"I need to get baptized, though, but Miss Cloverdale says that God will understand. But I don't want to meet Him without having obeyed Him. She says I need a pastor and deep water, but we don't have either one of those here."

"Well, I'm assistant pastor of the church, but Miss Cloverdale is right about the water."

That was when Grace saw the last thing the boy needed. "Brother Kweli," she said, "I believe there is a way."

The assistant pastor followed Grace's look and grinned when he saw it. "Why, I do believe you're right, Miss Cloverdale."

"Dr. Gray, wait," Grace said and grabbed Sam's arm to stop him. "Give him to Brother Kweli."

"Grace, what are you—" That's when Sam saw where Grace was looking. "He doesn't have time for this, do you hear me? His appendix could rupture at any moment!"

"Dr. Gray, it's all right," Grace said, turning her head to look up into Sam's warm, brown eyes. "Give him to Brother Kweli."

"Grace, this is *ridiculous*, and it could—"

"Dr. Gray, trust me," she said softly, her voice so calm and sure.

Sam handed the boy over to the waiting African man and watched like this was all a dream.

As though he was in a church baptistery, Brother Kweli went to the decorative fountain, Machupa in his arms, and carefully climbed in, seeming to give no thought to ruining his clothes and shoes nor caring about the looks he received from all the passersby. With Grace and Sam watching, Brother Kweli looked down at the grinning young boy. "Upon your public profession of faith in the Lord Jesus Christ, I baptize you, my brother, in the name of the Father, and of the Son, and of the Holy Ghost." Brother Kweli told the boy to hold his breath and cover his nose, and he complied. "Buried in the likeness of His death . . . " Brother Kweli submerged the child beneath the cold fountain water. "Raised in the likeness of His resurrection." And Brother Kweli brought the boy back up out of the water and then handed him back to Sam.

So it was that young Machupa was baptized in the hospital's fountain only a few minutes before undergoing an emergency appendectomy . . .

* * *

Grace and Sam were seated in separate chairs of the hospital waiting room, both of them awaiting news of how Machupa's appendectomy was going. It seemed to Grace that Sam was comfortable with the silence, but Grace herself was not, for she kept remembering how she'd yelled at Sam when he'd asked her where her faith was. She'd been afraid to lose Machupa, for whom she'd been praying faithfully, and had lost her temper, something she very rarely did. And the fact that she'd directed her anger at Sam, who had only been trying to calm her down, was something she couldn't let go. "I'm sorry, Dr. Gray," she said, breaking the silence.

Sam glanced over at Grace and saw something he'd never expected to see in her eyes: guilt. "Sorry? Sorry for what?"

"For yelling at you earlier when you were trying to calm me down when I panicked. I know there was no way you could've known that Machupa wasn't saved yet, but still, that did not justify me losing my temper. I'm very sorry for yelling at you that way."

Sam leaned forward and gave her a smile. "Grace, everyone loses their temper. You were afraid for his life, and people who are afraid often lose their tempers."

"Just because everyone else does it doesn't make it right," she pointed out.

Sam reached over and took one of her hands in his, giving it a gentle squeeze. "What does that verse say? 'For all have sinned'? That includes you, too, right? Okay, so you've lost your temper and took your anger out on someone who didn't deserve it. That means you're just like everyone else, but you knew that already."

"But, Dr. Gray, as a Christian, I'm supposed to refrain from doing things that will ruin my Christian testimony. I'm held to a higher standard because I know better, and yet I gave in to my anger anyway."

"Well, when a Christian does something wrong, what are they supposed to do to try to make it right again? Do you have to get saved again?"

"No, once someone has accepted Jesus into their hearts, they cannot lose their salvation, no matter what they do. One of my favorite passages of Scripture is about that very thing, actually. It's John 10:27-30, and in it, Jesus is speaking. He says, 'My sheep hear my voice, and I know them, and they follow me. And I give unto them eternal life; and they shall never perish, neither shall any man pluck them out of my hand. My Father, which gave them me, is greater than all, and no man is able to pluck them out of my Father's hand. I and my Father are one.' His sheep are those who have chosen to follow Him. In the verses, Jesus specifically says He gives us *eternal* life. But my favorite part is where He says 'neither shall any man pluck them out of my hand' and then goes on to say 'no man is able to pluck them out of my Father's hand.' Well, by man, He means human. That means you can't take me out of God's hand, but it also means *I* can't take *myself* out of His hand either, no matter what I do. I actually use this passage after leading someone to the Lord so they know they can never lose their salvation."

"Then what does a Christian do when they do wrong?" Sam asked and found that he was genuinely curious about the answer.

"If our sin is against God only, we are to pray and ask Him to forgive us, and He does. If our sin is against another person, we are to go to the person we've wronged and ask their forgiveness; and then we are to pray to God and ask forgiveness from Him also, for the sin we committed against the person was also being disobedient to God, since He commanded us to love one another."

"And what if the person won't forgive you?"

"That, we can't control. If the person is bitter and angry and refuses to forgive, that is their sin, not ours. We've done what we could do to make it right, and as far as God is concerned, the relationship between the sinner and Him is repaired once more."

"Okay, so you came to me and apologized to me like you were supposed to do. Did you pray and ask God to forgive you after you apologized to me?"

"Yes, I prayed silently after I told you I was sorry."

"Then, according to the Bible, you've done everything you're supposed to do, right?"

"Yes," she answered, "but I still don't have your answer yet."

"Answer?"

"Do you forgive me for yelling at you?"

Sam smiled at her and gave her hand another squeeze. "Grace, you never had to apologize to me. I've heard a whole lot worse before from patients' family members screaming at me to do something for their child, cursing me out, and we've even had to call the police a time or two back in the office where I normally work. You raising your voice at me during a tense situation is completely understandable. I'm not angry with you; I never was."

Grace looked into his smiling brown eyes and felt her heart flutter and her stomach turn flip flops inside of her, hyperaware of his warm hand covering hers. "'For if ye forgive men their trespasses, your heavenly Father will also forgive you,'" she quoted softly to him and returned his smile with one of her own. She watched as a serious expression came over his face, and she had the odd feeling that he was considering kissing her. Unwilling to see if her feeling would be confirmed, she gently pulled her hand out of his and then leaned back in her chair, breathing slowly and deliberately to calm her heart back down again.

* * *

Sam had been considering kissing her until she pulled away, and with the serious moment broken, he forced himself to regain control. "So, I know that you and your family have been here for four years," he began conversationally, "but I haven't heard what brought you here."

"About six years ago, Dad began to feel called to go to the mission field," she started to explain.

"Called?" Sam questioned.

"Yes, called by God. It's a drive to do a specific thing or go to a specific place, and it gets stronger and stronger until you can't ignore it. Praying about it only makes you feel the need even more. With Dad, he felt called to the mission field, and he knew God wanted him to come to Africa. Dad has always had a drive to help children and on a short trip here to see about where he could put a church, he discovered a great need to help the orphans in the area. Dad knew then what God wanted him to do, and so he appointed his assistant pastor as new pastor, which the congregation agreed upon, and then began raising the money he knew he'd need. While he was raising the money, I began to feel called to help him. I knew he'd need schoolteachers and someone to look after the children, and so, after praying a lot about it, I knew that God was calling me to come help my dad. It was the same way with Esther, too. It took two years to raise up enough money, and then we came and found the land, which already had the buildings on it. We've been here ever since."

"What about your mother? Did she not feel called to come?" Sam asked curiously.

"If she'd been alive, she would've come here with Dad, for when two are married, they become one. In fact, she would've loved it here. But my mother was killed by a drunk driver when Esther and I were fourteen. That is one reason I don't approve of consuming alcohol."

Sam had never particularly cared for alcohol, but he had occasionally had a few drinks when he'd had a difficult day at the office, though he'd never gotten behind the wheel even after just one. The look on her face and the tone of her voice, although not meant for him, made him feel as though he was just as guilty for her mother's death as the person who'd hit and killed her, and suddenly, he found himself promising silently never to take another drink as long as he lived. "I'm sorry; I didn't know about your mother."

Grace smiled and said, "It's all right. Besides, she's in Heaven and I know I'll see her again someday. I do miss her a great deal. She was so beautiful and gentle. I don't ever remember seeing her angry, and when you did something wrong, she looked at you with this disappointed look in her eyes, and it just made you want to beg her for forgiveness and—"

"—and do anything to regain her favor," Sam finished knowingly as he stared into Grace's faraway gaze.

Grace blinked and looked at Sam, surprised that he understood so well. "Yes, exactly. How did you know?"

Sam laughed softly, but instead of answering her, he asked, "So where did you get your eye color from anyway? I thought identical twins had the same eye color, too."

"Normally they do but stranger things have happened. As for where my eye color comes from, I would say it comes from God, but that isn't the answer you're looking for."

Sam watched as Grace took hold of a thin, gold chain around her neck and pulled it gently up and over her head. At the end of the gold chain was a large, oval-shaped locket, and he saw her open the locket before handing it to him. Sam took it from her and looked inside it. There were two pictures inside the locket, a man who looked vaguely familiar and Grace. "You have a picture of yourself in your locket?" he asked and looked up at her when she began to laugh.

"That isn't me," she said through her laughter. "That's my mother when she was around my age, and the man is my father. Those pictures were taken about a year after they were married."

"Wow," Sam said, and he looked back down at the picture of the woman, "your mother was a very beautiful woman." He glanced up at Grace then and dared to say what he was thinking. "You look just like her, Grace."

Her face grew hot and red at the compliment, and she looked down at her lap to hide her reaction, knowing he'd already seen it. Biting her lip nervously, she absently took a strand of her hair and began twirling it around her finger. "Thank you for saying so, but I don't look *exactly* like her," she said.

"Yes, you do. You even have her dimples, one at each corner of your mouth, and they show up every time you smile. Not even Esther has dimples," he said nonchalantly and saw her head jerk up to stare wide-eyed at him in surprise, her face still red from his compliment. "I like your dimples."

"I—I—" she stammered but nothing else would come out.

"However, it was your eyes I noticed first. I have never seen eyes that color. When I first saw you, still thinking you were Esther, I wondered how I could have missed those eyes before. I couldn't stop staring, you know. You probably thought I was crazy, huh?"

"Not crazy, just strange. I didn't . . . I didn't know that's why you were staring at me that day."

Sam chuckled and confessed, "It wasn't just that day. It's still difficult to look away from you when you're looking at me."

"I'm sorry; I didn't realize I was distracting you," Grace said and felt her heartbeat speed up at his words.

"I don't mind, Grace," he said softly to her and held her locket back out to her.

She cleared her throat nervously, took the locket back from him, put it back around her neck—tucking the locket back into the front of her dress—and decided a change of subject was needed. "So, what brought you here, Dr. Gray?"

"I suppose you might say I was called, too."

"You were? By whom?" she asked, surprised.

He grinned and answered, "By my boss. As I told your dad, my boss signed up for a humanitarian aid program to bring heath care to third world countries. He gets donations, both money and equipment, whenever he helps out the program by sending doctors to these countries, and because there's a lot of money involved, he can afford to give extra to the doctors he sends."

"So you're being paid for being here?" Grace asked, once more surprised.

"I've got bills to pay, just like everyone else."

"So you volunteered to come only because of the money?"

"I didn't volunteer to come. My boss told me it was my turn to come, and because he's my boss, I came. I wouldn't be here otherwise. I've got patients back at home, and I don't like abandoning them like this, even though my colleagues at the office where I work are perfectly capable of handling them. At first, I hated it here. It's hot; the people's living conditions are unsanitary, which only makes germs fester; and children are dying from preventable illnesses, which angers me. But then I reminded myself that I'm in a position to make their situation better and that if I hadn't been here, I would never have saved as many lives as I have." He smiled at her, looking into her eyes, and added, "And I would never have met you."

"So what about your parents? Where are they?" she asked, trying to ignore the heat in her cheeks.

"My dad was born and raised in L.A., and he met my mom there in college. That's also where I was born, and I lived there until I was nine when my parents got divorced. While my dad stayed in L.A., my mom moved to St. Louis, Missouri, which is where she was originally from, and she's still there."

"You live in St. Louis?" Grace asked, hardly believing what she was hearing.

"Yes, and my doctor's office is there, too."

"That's amazing," she said, her eyes wide. "I was born and raised in St. Louis, as were both of my parents. My father used to be pastor of the Lighthouse Baptist Church there until he was called to the mission field."

Sam laughed. "All these years, we've lived in the same city, and it took being in Africa to finally meet each other? That's incredible."

"So how long will you be here?" Grace asked and tried not to show the sadness she felt, knowing this would not be a permanent assignment for him. She tried to imagine him leaving and her going on with her life without him and found that, not only could she not picture it, but that she also didn't want to.

* * *

Feeling much the same way as Grace, although he wasn't aware of that, Sam bravely hid his feelings and answered. "I stay here until the powers that be inform me that it's time for us to go. It could be weeks; it could be months. I usually won't know until days before I'm supposed to go."

"And will you be going back to St. Louis once you leave here?"

"Not right away. Usually, the aid program has us visit several countries before we go back to our respective homes."

"I . . . I know the children will miss you coming around," Grace said and felt a lump growing in her throat. *And so will I*, she added silently in her mind.

"I'll miss seeing them, too," Sam said back to her, his voice soft as he stared at her. *But I'll miss seeing you most, Grace*, he thought to himself.

"Miss Cloverdale?" a man said in Swahili.

Grace looked up from Sam's brown eyes and saw a doctor come in. "Yes?"

"I'm Dr. Balewa, Machupa's surgeon," the man said and watched Grace and Sam stand to their feet. "I just wanted to come by and update you on how he's doing. He's come through the surgery just fine, and he's in recovery but still unconscious from the drugs. He'll need to stay here in the hospital so we can keep an eye on him and make sure he doesn't develop any complications; but he's a strong boy, and I think he's going to be just fine."

"Praise the Lord!" Grace exclaimed in relief. With that concern taken care of, another one took its place in her mind. "But what about . . . what about the cost?"

Before the surgeon could answer, Sam responded. "I'll pay for everything, don't worry."

"Dr. Gray, I couldn't ask you to do that!" Grace exclaimed.

"So don't ask me. I'm going to do it anyway. Dr. Balewa, where do I go to arrange for payments for his care?"

"Dr. Gray, you really don't have to do this."

"Don't worry, Grace; I can afford it."

"But there's no way we'll be able to pay you back," she explained to him.

Sam turned to look at the frowning woman beside him and smiled down at her. "I know that. Don't worry about it; I'm glad to help." He tilted his head curiously as he saw tears spill from her grateful eyes. He understood her gratefulness, but the tears confused him.

Having fought the sadness of thinking about him leaving Africa, when he decided to pay for Machupa's medical care, knowing the school couldn't afford to pay him back, Grace's heart swelled with relief that her student would be cared for. The tears she'd held back at the thought of Sam leaving now leaked out of her eyes, and try as she might, she couldn't stop them. "'He that hath pity upon the poor lendeth unto the Lord; and that which he hath given will he pay him again.' That's Proverbs 19:17, in case you didn't know," she said, knowing he didn't.

"What does it mean?" Sam asked, still wondering why she was crying.

"It means that by you helping Machupa, you're lending money to the Lord, so to speak; and what you give to the Lord, the Lord will pay it back to you," she explained.

Finally, he caught a sad look in her eyes but he couldn't imagine why she would be sad. To cheer her up, he said casually, "He doesn't have to pay me back either." He grinned when he was rewarded with her laughter. "Let me go take care of the payment arrangements. I'll be right back, okay?"

"Okay, and thank you for everything."

"Any time, Grace," he said softly. He began to follow the surgeon, but he couldn't resist looking behind him for one more look at her. He smiled when he saw her kneeling right there on the waiting room floor, her hands folded and her head bowed, her lips moving silently, and he knew she was thanking God.

* * *

"This is it," Grace said, pointing to a little white house with an aging white fence surrounding the yard, except for the gap left open to access the driveway.

Sam pulled into the dirt driveway and parked in behind a small, blue van. "Don't worry about your van. I'll drive it back here tomorrow when I come to give the kids their checkups, and Laura can drive my truck. If you'll give me the key and trust me enough to let me drive it, that is."

Grace unbuckled her seatbelt and collected her purse from the floorboard of the old pickup. Opening up her purse, she pulled out her key ring and took off the van key. Holding it out to him, she said, "Well, I think I can trust you, and I know you don't drive like a maniac. Except when it's an emergency anyway."

He laughed and took the key from her, straightening out his legs so he could put the key into his pants pocket.

"You want to come in?" Grace asked him.

"I would, but it's late, and I haven't eaten anything since lunch except that small snack in the hospital."

Grace's mouth dropped open and then, recovering, she asked, "You mean you missed dinner? Dr. Gray, why didn't you say anything? We could've gone down to the hospital cafeteria and eaten there!"

"I'm not a big fan of hospital food. It's okay, though; I'll eat when I get home. Won't take me too long to put some rice on, and I've got beans from last night's supper that I can heat up. That'll fill me up."

"At least come in long enough to eat something," Grace coaxed him.

"I wish I could—I really do—but I've got to get up early in the morning."

"And what do you plan to make for breakfast?"

"Probably the rest of tonight's dinner. Why?"

Grace got out of the truck and looked into Sam's curious brown eyes. "Wait right here, okay? I'll be right back."

"But—"

"Promise me you'll wait right here."

"I promise I'll wait," Sam said, wondering what had gotten into her.

* * *

Thomas had glanced at the clock when he heard a vehicle pull up outside and hoped it was Grace, for she should've been back long before now. He moved the curtain aside and looked out but didn't recognize the pickup he saw, so he figured someone was turning around in the driveway, which happened quite frequently. Going back to his Bible reading, he was startled when the front door burst open and he saw Grace come running into the house, tossing her purse onto the couch as she made her way to the kitchen. "Grace, honey, is anything wrong?" he called to her.

"Hold on, Dad!" she responded from the kitchen.

Thomas frowned as he heard the fridge being opened and then a bunch of clanging and shuffling noises. "Grace, what are you doing?"

"Give me a second, will you, Dad?"

Perplexed, Thomas listened to the noises coming from the kitchen, and before long, he saw his daughter come back in, still hurrying, and carrying three of their biggest microwaveable containers. "Grace?"

"I'll explain everything when I come back in, I promise," Grace told him and then went out the front door.

* * *

Sam waited patiently in the truck, and not long after she'd gone in, he saw her open the door and come back out, carrying something in her hands. He watched her come around to the driver's side, and when she got to him, she held her hands out.

"Here," she said to him, a huge smile plastered across her face.

Sam took what she offered and looked down to see three plastic food containers. "What is this?"

Grace pointed at the bottommost container and said, "That's for tonight's supper; the middle one is for breakfast; and the top one is dessert. And don't worry, I always make triple the recipe—because it goes fast—so we still have plenty for ourselves."

Sam set aside the breakfast and dessert containers before opening the dinner container. Immediately, his stomach rumbled as the delicious aroma reached his nose. "Is this lasagna?"

"It sure is," Grace said.

"And you say you made it?"

"I cooked it yesterday after school was over—made it for dinner tonight."

"It smells wonderful. I can't even remember the last time I had homemade lasagna." Sam closed it tightly and traded the dinner container for the breakfast container.

"I wasn't sure how many to give you, since I don't know how much you eat; so I gave you the same amount as my dad eats, since you and he have similar builds. I hope it'll be enough," Grace said and watched as Sam opened up the container he was holding.

Inside the container sat four large, golden brown waffles with fresh strawberries and blueberries on top of them. Sam looked up at

Grace and saw her blue-green eyes shining brightly in the darkness. "Are these homemade, too?"

"Yes," she answered. "Everything I cook is. It tastes better, and it's not like back in the States where I can run down to a grocery store and get something store-bought. I wasn't sure about the fruit. I eat them with the fruit and some maple syrup on them. Oh, that little container right there has the syrup. I didn't want the waffles to get soggy before you could eat them and I didn't know if you had any at your house. If you don't like the fruit, you can just pick them off of the waffles."

Sam heard nervousness in her voice for the first time since he'd met her and wondered the reason for it. He smiled at her and saw her bite her bottom lip as a finger went up and began twirling a strand of her hair just as she'd done in the hospital waiting room. "No, they look delicious. I can't wait to try them in the morning," he said and saw her face practically glow. Once again, he closed the container and then reached for the last one.

"I didn't know what kind of dessert you liked, so I gave you a choice. If one of them isn't to your liking, just bring it back with you tomorrow when you come to the school, and I'll make sure it won't go to waste."

Sam opened the dessert container, and his eyes grew wide as he saw what was inside. "A piece of chocolate cake with chocolate frosting and a piece of lemon meringue pie," Sam said and looked up from the container to stare into Grace's eyes. "I haven't seen food like this since I came here. Woman, I could kiss you right now, you know that?"

"What? Please, Dr. Gray . . . " she said, backing up a step, wringing her hands nervously.

Sam laughed at her reaction and said, "Don't worry, I won't. But this is just so thoughtful of you, Grace; it really is." Sam found he could not look away from her gaze, just as had been the case when he'd first seen her. As she stood there staring back at him, her finger once again twirling a stray strand of wheat-colored hair, he realized just how very dear she'd become to him. *I love her* came the thought unbidden into his mind, and the realization made it difficult for him to breathe. Her next words didn't help either.

"Well, with the long day you had at the tent and then I come along and keep you from your dinner, it was the least I could do. Besides, you don't have a wife to cook for you, so *someone's* got to feed you."

Sam saw the shock come over her face when she realized what she'd just said and then watched her face turn a deep red.

"I . . . I only meant that . . . "

"It's okay, I know what you meant," he said gently.

Grace shivered when she heard a softness in his tone that had not been there before. "I hope . . . I hope you enjoy the food, Dr. Gray. I'll see you tomorrow at the school."

He wanted to tell her, to take her in his arms and kiss her, to run his fingers through her long, silky hair, and to never let the moment end. Instead, knowing her well enough to know that she would not have welcomed such forwardness, he closed up the dessert container and then secured all three of them so they wouldn't shift during travel. Then he looked back into her eyes and said tenderly, "I'm looking forward to it, Grace." He threw the pickup into reverse and backed out of the driveway, then motioned for her to go inside. Once she had gone in and closed the front door behind her, he put the gear into drive and headed home, thoughts of Grace turning over in his head. *No more waiting,* he told himself. *I don't know how much time I have left to be here, and I'm not about to waste any more of it. I'll ask her out tomorrow. I don't have a clue where to take her, but I'm going to ask her anyway.* Then his mind went back to the thought he'd had, and he pictured her standing in her driveway staring at him as she twirled the strand of hair around her finger, waiting for his reaction to the food she'd given to him. "How in the world am I going to tell her that I love her?" he wondered aloud.

* * *

Grace shut the front door and locked it, then leaned her back against it, her thoughts racing and her heart pounding loudly in her ears. Grace had known by the look in his eyes that something had changed inside him. She had seen surprise and then tenderness come over his face, and then just before he'd left, she'd seen determination. That look in his eyes had warmed her heart, but it had also frightened her, too, and she just knew that it was only a matter of time before he would make his feelings known to her and she would have to give a response. *God please, please, I beg You to keep him from asking me until after he's saved! I don't want to have to hurt his feelings, and he won't understand why I would have to refuse! Please, God, don't let him ask me yet!*

"Grace?" Thomas called and saw his usually calm daughter startle, hearing her soft gasp of surprise.

"Oh, Dad, I'm sorry. I guess I got lost in my own thoughts."

"I could see that. Do I get that explanation now?"

"Explanation?"

"When you came rushing in, you promised you'd explain everything to me. Would you like to begin by telling me why you're so late getting home, where your van is, and whose truck that was parked in the driveway?"

"Machupa had appendicitis this morning, but I didn't know it at the time, so I rushed to the medical tent for help. Dr. Gray was just coming out, so he examined him and explained what was going on and said Machupa needed to be taken to the hospital. We got in the truck and . . . " Grace's voice trailed off when she recalled the feeling of Sam's hands lifting her up easily into the back of the pickup, marveling at how strong he was.

"You got in the truck and . . . what?" Thomas prompted when he saw Grace drift off.

Grace shook herself out of her reverie. "Sorry," she said. "Anyway, we got in the truck, and Dr. Gray drove to the hospital while I stayed in the back with Machupa. Well, Machupa had heard Dr. Gray mention what was going on, and he told me he didn't want to die and go to Hell. So right there in the back of the truck, I led Machupa to the Lord!"

"Praise the Lord! We've been praying for him for years to get saved!" Thomas said jovially.

"Well, we got to the hospital, and he was wanting to get baptized. But of course, he couldn't because we didn't have deep water or a pastor with us. He kept insisting, saying he didn't want to die without obeying God, so I explained to him that God wouldn't be angry and that He would understand. Next thing I know, Brother Kweli is coming out of the hospital entrance, calling to me. I asked him to call the church and start a prayer circle for Machupa's health, and then he told him he'd gotten saved and wanted to be baptized and explained why he couldn't. Brother Kweli mentioned he was assistant pastor and that's when I noticed the large fountain. So Machupa got baptized in the hospital fountain! You should've seen it, Dad!"

Thomas chuckled. "I wish I could have. That boy will be mightily used of God; I just feel it. Most kids don't have a drive to obey God that strongly. I'm happy for him and proud of him, too."

"I am, too. Well, Dr. Gray and I took Machupa into the hospital, and they confirmed the diagnosis and took him right into surgery as soon as they could. He came through it all right, but they're going to keep him until it's safe for him to come home."

"It'll be expensive. We can pray the money in, for I have no doubt that God will supply the need, but the hospital will—"

"It's been taken care of, Dad," Grace interrupted.

"What?"

"God already supplied the need. Dr. Gray made arrangements with the hospital. He's going to pay for whatever Machupa needs."

Thomas' brows shot up as his eyes widened. "That's very generous of him, but it will take a very long time to pay him back."

"He isn't asking to be paid back. I tried to talk him out of it, but he insisted. I explained we wouldn't be able to pay him back, and he said he knew that already. Anyway, we stayed at the hospital until Machupa woke up, and we got to talk to him a little bit. I told him that one of us would be back tomorrow to check on him, so he won't be by himself, but that we couldn't stay. Since my van is still at the medical tent parking lot, Dr. Gray drove me home. That was his truck you saw."

"Well, that explains all of those questions. Now would you like to tell me what you were doing in the kitchen?"

"Remember I said that as I'd gotten to the medical tent, Dr. Gray was standing outside in the parking lot?"

"I remember," Thomas said patiently.

"He'd just gotten off of work for the day, and he was on his way to get something to eat when I drove up needing help with Machupa. Well, I didn't realize it, and he never said anything until I asked him if he wanted to come in for a little while. He mentioned he needed to get home and eat something because he hadn't had anything since lunch. I told him he could come in to at least get something to eat, but he said he was really tired and needed to get home, that he had to wake up early in the morning. He said it wouldn't take him long to fix some rice, and he could eat some of the leftover beans he'd had at dinner the night before. I asked him what he was going to eat for breakfast, and he told me he'd eat whatever was leftover from tonight's dinner. Now, after everything he did for Machupa, I couldn't very well let him do that, now could I?"

"No," Thomas agreed, "no, you couldn't."

"Exactly, so I made him promise to wait for me, and I came in here and got him several big slices of lasagna and four waffles leftover from breakfast this morning. I topped the waffles with some fruit and then put some maple syrup in a little container because I didn't know if he had any. I was about to take it all out to him when I thought he might like to have some dessert, too; and since we had extra, I gave him a piece of chocolate cake and lemon meringue pie."

"Two pieces of dessert?" Thomas queried curiously.

"I didn't know what he likes, so I figured I'd give him one of each."

"That makes sense," Thomas said, nodding more to himself than to her. "And I'm glad you made sure he got some good food. I can't even imagine how difficult being a pediatrician is. You go get yourself some dinner now, and I'll call one of the men from church to meet me tomorrow to get the van."

"That's okay, Dad. Dr. Gray promised to drive it to the school tomorrow when he comes to give the kids their checkups. He's going to let the nurse drive his truck, and he'll bring the van. I went ahead and gave him the key."

Thomas saw worry in her eyes then and watched her twirl a strand of hair around her finger, a habit she had whenever something was bothering her. "You know," he said conversationally, closing up his Bible, "I could go for some dessert myself right about now. How about we continue this conversation in the kitchen, hmm?" He saw her meet his gaze, and he could tell that she knew what he was doing. In her usual no-nonsense style, she told him what was on her mind.

"Dad, I think he's going to ask me out soon."

Immediately, Thomas began to pray for wisdom so that he could advise his daughter properly. "What makes you believe that?" he asked slowly as he gathered his thoughts.

"I had this feeling tonight that he would, and even though he didn't, it isn't the first time I've felt it. It was so much stronger tonight, though."

"And how do you feel about him asking you out?"

"How do I *feel*?" she repeated. "Nervous, excited, anxious, and afraid all at once. And when he was looking at all the food I brought to him, I felt like if he rejected the food, it would be like he was rejecting me. I couldn't make up my mind whether that would be a good thing or a bad thing. Isn't that silly?"

"No, not really. I remember the first time your mother cooked for me, she was so worried that I'd hate her cooking that she couldn't stay in one place. Did Dr. Gray appreciate the food?" Thomas saw his daughter blush deeply at the question.

"He looked me straight in the eyes and said he hadn't seen food like that since he'd come here. And then he said . . . Oh, I don't know if I can even get the words out! I don't think he meant to say it, but I'm not sure. He said, 'Woman, I could kiss you right now, you know that.' I got so scared, I really thought he was going to! He didn't though, never even tried. Made me relieved but also . . . disappointed, too."

"So you wanted him to?"

"I wouldn't have let him—I know better than that—but . . . well, yes, I did want him to at least *try*. After he said that, he told me it was really thoughtful of me to give him the food. That's when he got this look in his eyes, and I had that feeling. I know he's going to ask, Dad; I have no doubt about it."

"Honey, he isn't saved," Thomas said gently and saw the pain in her eyes.

"I know," she said in a subdued tone of voice.

Thomas waited, knowing there was more she needed to say.

"Daddy, I need you to pray for me," she said, a desperate note in her voice.

"Do you want me to pray that he won't ask you out?"

"No," Grace said as more tears fell from her eyes. "I want you to pray that when he does ask me out, if he's still unsaved, that I'll have the strength to say no, no matter how much I love him. And I do, Daddy. I love him *so much* . . . " Then Grace broke down into tears and wept, her heart aching.

That night, Grace finished her nightly devotions, but her mind was still preoccupied with Sam, and she knew she'd never get any sleep. Her heart burdened for the man she loved, she knelt down next to her bed and prayed fervently for Sam's soul, begging God once more to bring Sam to salvation.

* * *

His stomach full from the homemade lasagna and the piece of apple pie he'd eaten for dinner, Sam felt satisfied for the first time in weeks, grateful to Grace for giving the food to him. Humming to himself, he got ready for bed, certain that all he'd needed was good food so he could get some sleep, attributing his lack thereof to going to bed hungry. Shutting off the light, he climbed into bed and pulled the covers on him, staring up at the darkened ceiling, recalling Grace once more and how he'd wanted to tell her that he loved her. "Don't rush it. She won't approve," he told himself aloud. "Just ask her out tomorrow and then go from there." With a short-term plan firmly in his mind, he closed his eyes and felt himself begin to drift off to sleep. Just before he could, however, her voice, gentle and reproving, began to echo inside his mind, a new phrase added to the others, and it kept him from getting to sleep.

"For the wages of sin is death. If you died today, do you know where you would spend eternity? You won't go to Heaven; you'll go to Hell! For the wages of sin is death. If you died today, do you know where you would spend eternity? You won't go to Heaven; you'll go to Hell! For the wages of sin is death . . . "

CHAPTER FOUR

*"Let your speech be alway with grace, seasoned with salt,
that ye may know how ye ought to answer every man."*

Colossians 4:6

GRACE WAS JUST ABOUT TO finish the Bible lesson for the day when she heard the expected knock at her door. Taking deep, measured breaths to calm her rapidly beating heart, she walked to the door and answered it, smiling when she saw Sam on the other side. As soon as she saw his eyes, a voice inside of her told her that it would be today. *No, God, please don't let him,* she prayed silently.

"Here," he said, holding out the food containers.

"Tell me you didn't eat all of the food already!"

Sam laughed and said, "No. I stored what was left in my own containers so I could bring you back yours."

"Thank you; I appreciate it," she said and moved to let him in. She walked to the desk to set the containers down on it and turned around to find that Sam had followed her.

"This is yours, too," he said and held out her van key. When she took the key from him and her fingers touched his, she felt warmth sweep through her.

"Thank you for bringing the van back to me," she replied and pulled open a bottom drawer to get her purse out. She pulled the key ring out of her purse and put the van key back on where it belonged then put her purse back into the drawer and closed the drawer back up. "I'm on the final part of today's lesson, so if you could wait for a bit, it won't take very long."

"Of course," Sam said and made his way over to the closest empty desk.

Grace waited until both Sam and the nurse were seated before she continued. "All right, class," Grace said, picking up a stack of papers from off of her desk, "today is test day." She smiled as she heard the groans from her students, and she began to pass out the test sheets. "Come on, now; everything on this test we've all been learning in class. Most of you know this by heart, so you shouldn't be worried." As she neared where Sam was seated, an idea came into her head, and she decided it was a good one. So when she reached his desk, she placed one of the test sheets down in front of him and then took a pencil out of her pocket and placed it on the desk, smiling when she heard her students laughing. "Today, class, we see how well you all have been paying attention to my lessons."

Sam looked up into her eyes and saw a challenge in them behind her smile just before she moved on to the rest of her students. *Does she honestly expect me to do this?* he wondered. *And what if I decide not to do it?* He had the feeling that it would make her disappointed, and he did not wish to see that expression upon her face, especially not today.

Grace finished handing out the papers and walked back to the desk, sitting down. "Remember, no cheating off of each other's papers, no talking, no passing notes, and bring your paper up to my desk and put it in the basket when you're finished. Does anyone need to sharpen their pencil before we begin?" She waited, but no one raised their hand. "Very well, then, class, you may begin." Grace saw her students begin at once on their papers, the soft sound of pencils being used clearly heard in the silence of the room. Looking to Sam then, she saw him watch her for just a moment before he picked up the pencil she'd given to him and began to fill out his own test paper. She had thought he wouldn't do it, and she knew that there were questions on the test that he probably would not be able to answer, but the fact that he would even attempt it caused her heart to overflow with joy and love for him, knowing that he was trying for her sake.

Grace set about grading homework papers as the minutes ticked by, and eventually, her students began to bring their finished papers up front to place them into the basket before returning to their desks to quietly pull out one of their books and read while they waited for the others. Halfway through her homework papers, she was interrupted when a test paper was placed directly over the paper she was currently grading. When she looked to see which student had done it, she found herself face to face with Sam. Grace moved her hand and looked down at the paper he'd given to her. When she saw what he had written at the top, she had to cover her mouth to stifle a laugh, for beside where it had the word "Name" printed, he'd written "Call me Sam!!!!" When she looked back up at him, she could see the laughter dancing in his eyes, and she couldn't help but smile at him. Taking her red pencil, she then proceeded to grade his test paper while waiting for the last of her students to finish their work. As she read his answers, it surprised her to see how many he'd gotten correct—more than she'd thought he would have—proving that he'd actually been listening to the lessons instead of just staring at her or tuning the words out. After she had looked the entire paper over, she handed it back to him and suppressed a smile when he looked curiously for the grade just like any regular student would have.

Oddly anxious to know how well he did, Sam looked at the paper and was shocked when he saw the grade. She'd printed a great big letter B and had circled it so that he would not miss it. Below that, she'd written in the loveliest penmanship he'd ever seen, *So you have been paying attention after all. Well done, Dr. Gray!* He chuckled softly, knowing why she'd underlined his name, and he looked down at her, grinning at her. When she grinned back, he saw her mouth the words, "Thank you." He knew she was thanking him for humoring her, so he gave her a quick wink and grinned wider when he saw her blush. Then he went back to his seat and sat down to wait for the students to finish their work so that he could begin their checkups, feeling confident and happy.

That afternoon after school had been dismissed, Grace finished grading the last of the papers and then moved to tidy up the classroom. Alone with time to think, her mind went back to that morning and she felt grateful that Sam had not asked her out, for when she'd seen him, she had thought for sure that he intended to do so. She took a spray can of wood polisher and a roll of paper towels and began wiping down the students' desks, a soft smile on her face as she remembered how Sam had taken the test and how well he had done, her smile widening when she remembered reading what he'd put for his name. She began to hum then, and when she finished wiping down all of the desks, she put the wood polisher up and got the spray bottle of disinfectant. Setting both the disinfectant and the paper towels on her desk, she went to the chalkboard, grabbed an eraser, and began to wipe the day's activities off, the smile still on her face and still humming contentedly to herself. Right after she'd finished that, she was about to place the eraser back down and get the disinfectant and paper towels when she heard an all-too familiar voice from behind her.

"Grace?"

She jumped, startled, and dropped the eraser, whirling around to face him, seeing him standing in her doorway with his eyes watching her, a serious expression in them. *No, please, God, send him away! Make him leave! Don't make me do this, please; Father, I beg You!* she prayed. "D-Dr. Gray, you startled me," she said nervously and then bent down to pick up the eraser.

"I'm sorry, I didn't mean to," he said quietly.

Grace turned her back on him, and with a trembling hand, she put the eraser back on the chalkboard tray. "Is something wrong with one of the children?" she asked, knowing already that this visit had nothing whatsoever to do with the children.

"No, the kids are doing quite well," Sam said and watched her rip off a paper towel from the roll on her desk and then grab the canister of disinfectant.

"That's good," Grace said and sprayed down the blackboard with the disinfectant, trying to keep from looking at his face. "Did you forget something when you were here earlier?"

"No," he answered and watched as she began to wipe down the blackboard. He walked over to where she was. "No, I need to talk to you about something."

"Well, I'm almost done here, Dr. Gray, and I need to go home and start dinner. Can it wait?" *Please, God, send an interruption, make him wait, something! Anything!*

"It's important," he said but she didn't stop wiping down the blackboard. "Grace, can you please stop cleaning—at least until I've told you what I came to tell you?"

"I really do have to finish this and go home," she told him. "And besides, you shouldn't be in here with me alone. Don't you remember what I told you the last time you were here?"

"Yes," he said. "You told me not to close the door, and I didn't."

"Well, yes, I did say that, but I also said you and I shouldn't be alone together even with the door open. Whatever it is you have to tell me can wait until next week. I—" The words died in her throat when he gently took the paper towel from her hand, and she turned around just in time to see him toss it onto her desk. *Please, God, send Dad or Esther into the room!* Grace honestly expected one of her family members to walk into the classroom just then and interrupt, but it was not to be.

"Grace, this can't wait."

I don't want to do this! I love him; I don't want to hurt him! Why, oh, why did I let myself love an unsaved man?! Hiding her trembling hands behind her back, she took a deep breath and prayed for strength and guidance, finally understanding that she was not going to get out of this easily. With a calm she did not feel, she said quietly, "All right, Dr. Gray. What is it you need to talk to me about?"

"I've been thinking about this for a while, but last night, I finally made up my mind to do it. I want to say that I think you're a wonderful woman; and I like how kind you are to everyone, how good you are with the kids, and how patient you are with me. I was wondering . . . I was wondering if you'd go out on a date with me."

She wished she could turn back time and stop him from saying the words. She wished that God had sent an interruption, wished to be anywhere but standing before him as he looked into her eyes and waited for her answer. *I would give anything to tell you yes, Sam,* she thought at him. Instead, she said miserably, "I can't, Dr. Gray."

* * *

He saw sadness and regret plainly in her blue-green eyes and knew he hadn't imagined her interest in him, so he couldn't understand why she would say no. "You could bring Esther or your dad along if you're worried about your reputation—I really don't mind— and we can go wherever you want."

"I'm sorry, but I really can't," she said and felt her heart aching at the confusion in his eyes.

"Do you already like someone else?" he asked and saw her flinch at the question.

"No, Dr. Gray, there is no one else," she answered softly.

"Do you just not like me then?"

"Of course I like you, Dr. Gray," she said.

"Then why won't you go out with me?"

She was about to explain gently to him why, but the Holy Spirit had other plans, and instead, she found herself quoting an often-used Bible verse. "'Be ye not unequally yoked together with unbelievers: for what fellowship hath righteousness with unrighteousness? and what communion hath light with darkness.'" As soon as the words were out of her mouth, she saw pain leap into his eyes, saw the confusion turn into anger, and knew she'd hurt him. She wanted to tell him she was sorry but she couldn't because what she'd said was the truth, and she couldn't apologize for being truthful.

"Darkness," he said, his voice barely above a whisper.

"Dr. Gray, what it means is—"

"Darkness," he repeated woodenly.

"Dr. Gray, please if you'll just let me explain—"

"Oh, you don't need to explain," Sam said stiffly, his voice hardening.

"No, wait, please, Dr. Gray, don't leave like this!" she exclaimed when he turned to leave.

"I'm sorry to have bothered you with my 'darkness,'" he said as he stopped in the doorway without bothering to look back at her. "I promise it won't happen again, Miss Cloverdale."

The use of her last name said so coldly was what finally caused her to begin crying. "Please, Dr. Gray, don't leave! Let me explain!" she begged, following as he left the room. "Please, would you just listen to me! Please! Dr. Gray, *please!*"

Sam said nothing; he just continued to walk toward the door, the Bible verse ringing in his ears, stinging painfully.

"*Dr. Gray, please!*" she called out, her tone becoming desperate, tears streaming down her face. She tried one more time, praying he would come back, praying it would be enough to stop him from leaving so that she could explain. "*PLEASE, DON'T GO, SAM!*" she shouted.

Sam never even slowed down and when he got to the double doors, he shoved one open angrily and walked out, her cries falling on deaf ears.

Her heart breaking, Grace reached out blindly for the doorway, her knees weak, and she felt like she was suffocating. "Don't go, Sam," she whispered as she wept. "I love you."

Esther had been in her classroom when she heard the shouting, and she stepped out into the hallway to see her sister slide down against her classroom doorway to the floor. "Grace!" Esther exclaimed and rushed over to where her sister sat on the floor, squatting down in front of her. "Grace, what's wrong? Why are you crying?"

Grace wrapped her arms tightly around herself and began to rock, unable to see anything except the pain that had been in Sam's warm brown eyes that she loved so much. "Sam's *gone!*" she cried out. "I love him, and he's *gone!*"

Never having seen her calm, collected sister this way, Esther couldn't imagine what might have happened between Grace and Sam, so not knowing what else to do, Esther sat on the floor and wrapped her arms around her distraught sister. "It'll be okay, Grace," Esther said soothingly. "He'll come back; you'll see."

"I love him, and he's *gone!*" Grace said again, and then she could only weep bitterly against her sister's shoulder, feeling like she was dying inside.

* * *

Thomas looked up from the sermon notes he was working on for the upcoming Sunday service when he heard the front door open. He frowned when he saw both of his daughters come into the house. "Well, good afternoon, you two. You're both home early today." Thomas saw Esther glance at him, worry on her face, but Grace just looked straight ahead as though she saw nothing. Thomas looked closer at Grace and saw she was crying. "Grace, honey, what's the matter?"

"Not now, Dad, please," said Esther quietly. Then to Grace, she said, "Come on, sis; I'll take you to your room, and you can rest. Dad and I will take care of dinner tonight."

Thomas watched as Esther led Grace to the hall, and after a little bit, he saw Esther returning alone to sit on the couch, sighing tiredly. "Esther, what's going on with Grace?"

"I was in my classroom straightening it up at the end of the day when I heard her shouting. When I walked out into the hallway, I found her on the floor in the doorway of her classroom crying. I asked her what was wrong, and she said that Sam was gone. Then she said she loved him and that he was gone. I tried to tell her that it would be okay, that he'd come back; and she just repeated that she loved him, and he was gone. I don't know what happened between them, Dad. I haven't been able to get anything else out of her, and she hasn't stopped crying. I've never seen her like this before. What do you suppose happened?"

"I imagine he told her how he felt about her, and she was forced to reject him because he's still unsaved."

"But, why? Why would he just leave? I know he cares about her; I *know* it."

"I don't doubt that, Esther; but you have to remember that no matter how gently Grace put it, being rejected still hurts. With Sam being unsaved, he wouldn't understand why she had to reject him, and it could cause him to be angry and bitter. We'll just need to pray for both of them, sweetheart."

"What if I went and talked to him tomorrow?"

"No, Esther, it's between the two of them, and we shouldn't interfere. Just keep praying, and everything will work out for the best."

"I just hate seeing her like this, Dad," Esther said sadly.

"I know, sweetheart," Thomas said. "I do, too, but we've got to trust God in this."

* * *

That night, Grace opened her Bible, got her prayer list, took her ink pen, crossed out Machupa's name from the "Unsaved" column, and then wrote it in the "Other" column, knowing he would need God's guidance as a new Christian always did. Once she was done revising her prayer list, she began to pray for those on it; but she found it difficult, for she would have to pause every once in a while to wipe her eyes so she could see what she was reading. She had not stopped crying since Sam had left her classroom, and she wondered if she would ever run out of tears. Shaking her head to clear it of thoughts, she went back to her praying and somehow managed to finish. Normally reading four chapters a night in her Bible, she managed only one before she closed the Book, unable to concentrate. Exhausted and heartbroken, she climbed into her bed, lay down, covered up, and tried to go to sleep. All she could do, however, was cry, soaking her pillow with her tears.

* * *

Sam had gone through the rest of his day feeling hurt and confused, reviewing all of the times he'd spent with Grace and how he was so sure she'd been interested in him just as he was in her. *How could she do that to me? How could she pretend to be interested and then blow me off like that?* he thought to himself, angry at her for leading him on, angry at himself for falling for it. That's when Tanya's words came back to him, then, reminding him that he'd been warned but had not bothered to listen to his friend.

"You should forget about her. She won't want anything to do with you. If you try to pursue a relationship with her, you'll just get your heart broken. You realize that, right?" she'd said.

"Why, Grace?" he asked aloud, uncomprehending. "Why would you do this? I don't understand!" Then he remembered how she'd shouted for him to come back, begged him not to leave, wanting him to listen to her, but he'd been so hurt and angry that he hadn't. When he'd heard her shout his name, he'd almost turned back to her then, but the pain she'd caused him was just too much, and he could not have faced her. Sitting at his little table, he put his head in his hands, feeling hollow inside. "How could you hurt me like this, Grace?" he whispered hoarsely. *"How?"*

Her face came to him then, eyes full of sadness, and when she spoke, he half expected it to be some kind of explanation dreamed up from his pain-filled mind. He was so very wrong.

"For the wages of sin is death, Sam. If you died today, do you know where you would spend eternity, Sam? You wouldn't go to Heaven; you'd go to Hell, Sam. For the wages of sin is death, Sam. If you died today—"

"SHUT UP!" he screamed suddenly and held his hands firmly against his ears. "SHUT UP AND LEAVE ME ALONE!" It didn't help, though.

"—do you know where you would spend eternity, Sam? You wouldn't go to Heaven; you'd go to Hell, Sam. For the wages of sin is death, Sam. If you died today, do you know where you would spend eternity, Sam? You wouldn't go to Heaven; you'd go to Hell, Sam. For the wages of sin is death, Sam . . . "

CHAPTER FIVE

"Let no corrupt communication proceed out of your mouth, but that which
is good to the use of edifying, that it may minister grace unto the hearers."

Ephesians 4:7

ALL THROUGHOUT THAT WEEK, GRACE prayed that God would
continue to work on Sam's heart, both to convict him of his need
for salvation and to soften it toward her again. She had decided that
when he came back to school to treat the children, she would send
the kids out to play for an early recess while she explained to him
that she hadn't refused him because she didn't want to go out with
him but that she couldn't go against her beliefs. She knew there was
a chance he wouldn't listen, knew that even if he did listen, it would
only make him angrier, but she knew she had to try to fix this if
she could, to make him understand that she hadn't been trying to
be mean or hurtful to him. So as the week went by slowly, Grace felt
the comfort of the Holy Spirit reminding her that no matter what
happened, everything would work out for the best; and although she
sometimes found herself wiping away tears from her eyes when the
pain became too much to bear, she kept telling herself that God had
a plan, and all she needed to do was trust Him to know what was best
for her.

So it was that on the following Friday, the day Sam would perform the checkups on the kids, Grace found it difficult to concentrate on the Bible lesson she was giving to the children, her ears attuned to the sound of knocking on her door, her heart racing with anticipation and fear, her finger constantly twirling a lock of hair as she waited for him to arrive, praying that he would hear and listen to what she had to say to him. She was halfway through her lesson, right in the middle of a Bible verse, when she heard a sharp rapping upon her door, which caused her to startle. Ignoring the children's laughter at her reaction, she placed her Bible carefully down on her desk and then walked over to the door. Taking a deep breath, she smoothed down her gray, polyester, circle skirt and then opened the door.

Behind the door stood a man in his late thirties with a shiny, bald head; thin salt-and-pepper hair on the sides and back of his head; a square-shaped face; wide nose; and small, steel blue eyes staring back at her from behind thin, wire-framed glasses. He wore a gray business suit; thin, black dress socks; and black penny loafers.

Grace had never seen this man before, and so when she spoke, her tone was all business, as it always was with strangers. "May I help you, sir?" she asked neutrally.

"I'm hoping so, miss," the man replied in a thick upper-class British accent. "Is this the fourth grade classroom? I was told to come here first."

"Yes, it is. Who are you?"

Both Grace and the stranger heard a nearby door open, and Grace saw Esther come out of her room and saw her sister startle at finding the man in the hallway; and when Esther looked to Grace, Grace just shrugged.

The stranger never even bothered to turn around, and so he did not see Esther behind him. "I'm Dr. Edward Williamson. I came with the rest of the physicians as part of the humanitarian aid program."

Grace frowned and said, "I don't understand. Why are you here, Dr. Williamson?"

"Why, I'm a pediatrician. I'm here to administer checkups for all of the children you have here."

Grace swallowed nervously, fear creeping into her heart. "But Sa—Dr. Gray—has been doing all the checkups on the children," she protested.

"Yes, I know. He's the one who sent me out here," Dr. Williamson said. "He told me to check the children in fourth grade first since they've been the sickest of all of the children. He also gave me a list of what medicines to give which child. You needn't worry, young lady."

"But I—I don't understand. Why would Sa—Dr. Gray—send you out here instead of coming himself?" Grace asked, utter confusion on her face.

"I'm not sure, but he was muttering some nonsense about darkness," he replied and didn't notice when Grace's face went pale as a ghost and her hand reached for the doorframe to steady herself. "Since last week, he hasn't been himself at all. I tell you, it's because of that missionary's daughter; I just know it is."

"M—missionary's daughter?" Grace repeated, only half-listening to the man's words.

"Yes, the Cloverdale woman. Not the chatterbox but the stodgy one."

Behind him, Esther stiffened, her hazel eyes narrowing, not at all appreciating this man referring to her sister as "the stodgy one."

"Wh-what do you mean he hasn't been himself all week? And why would you think it was because of her?" Grace asked.

"Well, he hasn't been sleeping well since he got here; but this past week, his behavior has gotten much worse, like he's walking around in some kind of trance or something, not really paying attention to anything. We've tried to give him some sleeping pills to help him, but he just ignores us all. And in addition to that, he's not eating as he should be. If he keeps this up, he'll make himself sick."

Oh, Sam, she lamented sadly. "Why do you think it was because of that missionary's daughter?" she pressed.

"Well, on Monday, he arranged for me to take over coming here; and when I asked him why, he said something about not troubling 'her' with his darkness anymore, whatever that means. I didn't have to ask who he meant by 'her' every one of us could see it on his face. I swear, someone should sit down and have a chat with that woman for what she's done to Sam. She is cold-hearted that's what she is! Imagine, a missionary's daughter leading Sam on and then breaking his heart when all he ever did was love her!"

Grace's eyes flew open, and she gasped loudly, her mouth dropping open at the stranger's words. "What did you just say?" she asked, afraid she hadn't heard correctly.

"I said she is cold-hearted for leading poor Sam on and then breaking his heart when all he ever did was love her," Dr. Williamson repeated firmly.

Grace grabbed the lapels of the British man and stared into the man's shocked face. "Are you sure? Are you *sure* he loves her?"

"Well, of course I am. It's written plainly across his face! All anyone has to do is look at him to see it!"

Grace released him, her mind racing, and ran back into her classroom, yanking open a bottom drawer to her teacher's desk and pulling out her purse. Running back toward the door, she pushed past Dr. Williamson and threw a glance at her twin. "Esther, watch my class!"

"I will, Grace!" Esther called back, a grin spreading wide across her face as she watched her sister run for the double doors just as fast as she could.

Dr. Williamson finally turned to see the person behind him and gave a start when he saw her. "But you—" he began and then looked to where the woman he'd been conversing with was just reaching the doors. "And she—" he tried again. He shook his head to clear it and then said, "Twins!" Then he remembered that the missionary's daughters were twins, and as he reviewed his words, he realized he'd been rather rude. "Which one are you?" he asked.

"I'm the chatterbox," Esther said ungraciously, the smile disappearing from her face as she stared at the man before her. "The one you were speaking with was the stodgy one."

"Oh, dear me, I didn't mean to insult either of you. It's just what everyone in the office calls you to keep you both separate when we're speaking of you. It's merely a descriptive."

"Uh huh," Esther said, unconvinced.

"Forgive me; I don't know your name."

"I'm Esther," Esther said stiffly, her voice cold, "but *you*, sir, may call me 'Miss Cloverdale.'"

* * *

Grace pulled up to the medical tent, parked the van, shut the engine off, collected her purse, and then got out, slamming the door shut and rushing for the tent's entrance. She walked in and went straight to the receptionist, whom she recognized.

"Miss Cloverdale! It's good to see you again!" Laura said as soon as she saw Grace.

"Laura, I need to see Dr. Gray. It's important," Grace said.

"It's not one of the children again, is it?" Laura asked, concern written across her face.

"No, nothing like that. But I need to speak with him," Grace said and saw the nurse relax.

"I'm sorry, Miss Cloverdale, but I can't let you go back there without signing in for a checkup or something."

"Well, where do I sign in?"

"Miss Cloverdale, Sam is a pediatrician. The best I can do is to have you see Dr. Tanya Grayson. She's one of our general practitioners, and she happens to be free at the moment."

"No, I've got to talk to Dr. Gray, and this can't wait any longer," Grace said, her voice betraying the distress she was feeling.

"Unless it's for a child, I'm afraid you'll have to wait until he gets off work later this afternoon," Laura said, feeling sorry for the upset woman.

"What . . . what if you put down one of my student's names? Obviously, none of my students are here, but . . . I *really* need to talk to him!"

"That will work, at least until he notices that you're not a child," Laura replied and handed Grace the sign-in clipboard and a pen. "Here, sign the child's name in and then have a seat. He's got three others ahead of you, so it'll be a little while, but it's the best I can do for you."

"Thank you! Thank you so much!" Grace said, relieved. Taking the clipboard and pen, Grace read the words "PLEASE PRINT" at the top of the page, and noting how those who'd signed in before her had done it, she went to the topmost blank line to write "Aadila Akintola—sick visit." Then, handing the clipboard and pen back to Laura, she looked at the nurse and said, "Don't tell him it's me. I'm . . . I'm afraid he wouldn't see me if he knew."

"I won't say a word," Laura promised. Then she read the name and grew concerned, looking back up at Grace. "Miss Cloverdale, if you're sick, I could—"

"It isn't that kind of sickness, Laura," Grace said, hoping the woman would understand.

"I see," the nurse said, nodding. "You may be just what the doctor ordered, then, Miss Cloverdale." Then Laura smiled and watched as Grace smiled back.

"I'm hoping so," Grace said. Feeling afraid, Grace went to sit down in one of the far chairs and began to silently pray, hoping God would give her the right things to say that would mend this rift that had grown between her and Sam. Only a few minutes after she'd sat down, she saw him pull the tent divider aside, come over to the desk, look at the clipboard, and call out a name without even bothering to look up. She was shocked when she saw his face, for there were bags and dark circles under his eyes and worry lines that had not been there the last time she'd seen him. When the child was brought up by his parent, Sam did not even bother to smile. *Oh, Lord, he looks so lost! Please, God, help him!* she prayed, hurting to see him like that.

Finally, after about a forty-five minute wait, Grace saw Sam come back, go to the clipboard, and call out the name she'd written.

"Aadila Akintola," Sam called and then set the clipboard back down, missing Laura's odd look.

Grace approached him and said simply, "That's me." She frowned when he didn't pay attention or even look at her, just turned and went to the tent partition that divided the waiting room from the rest of the tent. Grace followed him silently as he led her to a little room, moving aside another partition and walking inside. When both of them were inside, she scanned the room quickly before sitting down in one of the folding chairs as he went to use some hand sanitizer, his back turned to her.

"So, I saw on the sign-in sheet that this is a sick visit," Sam began in Swahili, rubbing his hands together to disinfect them. "What seems to be the matter?"

"My heart," Grace said softly in English. She watched as Sam immediately went rigid and then slowly turned around to face her.

* * *

"I don't have time for games, Miss Cloverdale," Sam said sternly and saw her flinch as though she'd been struck when he addressed her formally. He watched as her beautiful eyes glistened with unshed tears, and somehow, he managed to keep from going to her to comfort her, though it was difficult. He had missed seeing her face, hearing her voice, and staring into those Caribbean eyes he loved so much.

"It isn't a game, Dr. Gray," she said to him sincerely.

"I'm a pediatrician," he reminded her, his voice only just a little softer than before.

"I know, but you're also a general practitioner. You can diagnose heart trouble, too."

Sam took the stethoscope out of his doctor's coat and wrapped it around his neck. Then he walked to the stool and sat down on it. "What symptoms have you been having, and when did you first notice them?"

Grace relaxed slightly, breathing out the breath she hadn't realized she'd been holding until then. "Well, I first noticed it about five weeks ago," Grace said. "My heart would start to beat faster, and I'd feel kind of . . . odd. As time went by, I'd have moments where I found it difficult to breathe, but they never lasted very long, and my heart would race. Usually, I could calm myself down if I took slow breaths in and out, but the more time passed, the worse it seemed to get. Then I started hearing a pounding in my ears whenever this happened. It wasn't so bad until last week, when I felt this horrible, sharp pain in my chest. I . . . I felt like I was dying."

As Grace had spoken, Sam grew concerned for her, and when she described the sharp pain in her chest, he became downright alarmed. He stood to his feet, walked over to her, put his stethoscope in his ears and then placed the flat part on her back. "Take several deep breaths for me," he said, and he listened to her lungs. Satisfied that they were fine, he went and retrieved the blood pressure cuff and came back. "Hold your arm out."

"Dr. Gray, about last week—" she began, but he immediately stopped her.

"Forget about last week," he said dismissively. "I'm more worried about your heart. Hold your arm out."

Grace saw then the fear in his eyes, and she realized what she'd done. "But—"

"Hold your arm out, or I'll take you to the hospital," Sam said firmly.

Grace held her arm out and watched his expression as he put the cuff on her, a small smile lifting the corners of her lips at how concerned he was for her even though she'd hurt him.

Sam finished taking her blood pressure. "Well, your blood pressure is elevated but not alarmingly so." He set aside the blood pressure cuff and then put his stethoscope back in his ears, taking the flat end. "Okay, now let's see if I can hear a heart murmur or . . . "

When Sam moved the flat part of the stethoscope toward her heart, Grace grabbed his hand before he got very far. "Listen, I need to say something to you. I—"

"Why didn't you get help for this earlier? You should've said something to me or made an appointment," he chastised.

"Because it didn't hurt before," she said honestly.

"That's no excuse! You could have a serious heart problem; do you realize that? It could be a heart murmur, or it could be an arterial blockage or a—"

"It's not that kind of heart problem," she said calmly, her eyes watching his.

The phrase jogged his memory, and he remembered her father saying something similar to him upon their first greeting.

"You say you're a doctor, too? What do you specialize in, if you don't mind me asking?" Sam had asked the older man.

"Oh, I don't mind at all. My specialty is the heart," Thomas had answered.

"A cardiologist, eh? Odd that I don't remember seeing you on the plane with the rest of my colleagues," Sam had remarked.

Thomas had chuckled and replied, *"I'm not that kind of heart doctor, young man. I'm a pastor and missionary."*

Jolting back to the present, Sam asked her, suspicious now, "What do you mean it's not that kind of heart problem?"

"'Stay me with flagons, comfort me with apples: for I am sick of love,' Song of Solomon 2:8," Grace quoted softly.

Sam's eyes narrowed, his anger returning, and he said, "I told you, I don't have time for games."

Undaunted, Grace continued, "'Tell me, O thou whom my soul loveth, where thou feedest, where thou makest thy flock to rest at noon: for why should I be as one that turneth aside by the flocks of thy companions?' Song of Solomon 1:7."

"Miss Cloverdale, I am a very busy man, and I don't have time to—"

"'I opened to my beloved; but my beloved had withdrawn himself, and was gone: my soul failed when he spake: I sought him, but I could not find him; I called him, but he gave me no answer,' Song of Solomon 5:6!" Her shoulders began to shake as tears finally began to drip from her eyes. "'I charge you, O daughters of Jerusalem, if ye find my beloved, that ye tell him, that I am sick of love,' Song of Solomon 5:8!"

"*Miss Cloverdale . . .*" he said firmly, his anger now full-blown.

* * *

She could hear the anger in his voice, see it in his eyes, but she wasn't about to give up. "'The voice of my beloved! behold, he cometh leaping upon the mountains, skipping upon the hills,' Song of Solomon 2:8," she interrupted him. With trembling hands, she touched his face and placed her thumbs upon his eyelids. "'His eyes are as the eyes of doves by the rivers of waters, washed with milk, and fitly set,' Song of Solomon 5:12."

When she moved her thumbs, he looked into her eyes then and saw fear, uncertainty, and a vulnerability that he'd never seen in her before and her hands upon his face felt as though they burned through his skin. He opened his mouth to speak, not knowing what he was about to say, but she beat him to it.

Tears streaming down her cheeks, Grace kept a firm though gentle grasp of his face, and staring into his eyes, she said, "'It was but a little that I passed from them, but I found him whom my soul loveth: I held him, and would not let him go,' Song of Solomon 3:4a."

Those words "him whom my soul loveth," said so tenderly and sincerely rang in his ears, and he finally understood what she'd been trying to tell him. "Grace," he said softly and watched as she began to weep uncontrollably.

She once more quoted the verse she had begun with, knowing that this time he would understand what she meant. "'Stay me with flagons, comfort me with apples: for I am sick of love,'" she whispered to him in a wavering voice.

"Oh, Grace," he said tenderly and began to gently wipe away the tears from her face, but it seemed to only make her cry harder; so instead, he wrapped his arms around her and held her against him, stroking her soft, golden brown hair and breathing in her sweet scent.

"I never meant to hurt you, Sam!" she cried. "The verse just came out of me, and when I saw your face, I knew you'd taken it the wrong way; so I tried to explain but you . . . you—"

"I wouldn't listen," he supplied quietly and shut his eyes to the pain in her voice.

"And it hurt so much to see you walk away from me like that, and I cried all day and the whole night, too. Every time I tried to go to sleep, I kept seeing the hurt in your eyes! So the next morning, after I prayed about it, I decided to tell you when you came back to the school to give the kids their checkups. I even planned to send the kids to early recess just so I could talk with you! I looked forward to fixing it, to explain everything and make you understand that I wasn't trying to hurt you. And then today, when I heard that knock on the door, I was so nervous but determined that I would not leave things like they've been all week. But when I opened the door, it wasn't you. When I asked why he was there, he told me you'd sent him and that you weren't coming back, and I . . . I . . . "

She broke down sobbing again, and Sam tightened his hold on her, realizing only now how stupid he'd been to believe that she had ever been pretending with him. "I am so stupid," he said to himself, guilt eating him up inside for thinking she'd ever been anything but honest with him. "I should've known better; I should've stayed to hear you out, or at least turned back around when you shouted my name. That was stupid of me, Grace. I'm so sorry."

"It's all right, Sam; I understand why you didn't, and I forgave you the moment you did it," she assured him.

He chuckled then and said, "I don't know how you can forgive so easily when you've been hurt like this but you always seem to. That . . . that's one of the things I love about you, Grace."

She moved far enough away to meet his gaze and asked, "*Do* you love me, Sam? That doctor you sent, he said you did, but that doesn't mean anything. It could just be gossip, and I don't trust gossip."

Sam used his right hand to wipe more of her tears away, and then he caressed her cheek, finding it soft and smooth to the touch. "I've loved you from the moment I laid eyes on you, Grace," he told her, "and the more I got to know you, the more I loved you." He watched as her eyes lit up and sparkled wildly as a smile spread across her lips. He could see it now in her eyes, the truth that she loved him, too. *If only I had turned around when she'd called my name, I would've seen it and known then and saved us both this horrible week,* he thought to himself. His heart near to bursting with love for her, he leaned toward her then, intending to kiss her as he'd wanted to do for so long. He was stopped by her palm putting gentle pressure on his chest.

"Sam, what are you doing?" she asked, though she could guess.

"I'm going to kiss you, of course," he answered, thinking that it should've been obvious.

"I don't want you to kiss me," she said before she thought. She frowned then at her own words and shook her head. "No, that's not what I meant. I *do* want you to kiss me, but we can't."

"But why not?" he asked, confused again.

Grace stood up and moved away from him then, knowing she needed a clear head in order to explain things to him. "Sam, if I explain, will you hear me out this time?"

He saw her bite her lip and start to twirl a lock of her hair around one of her fingers, and he realized she was nervous. "I will. I promise."

"When you asked me out, I wanted to say yes. I've known for a while that I loved you, and I wanted so badly to spend more time with you. But I can't have a relationship with you, no matter how much I love you and no matter how much I want to."

"Because of my darkness," he said knowingly.

"Because you aren't saved," she rephrased gently.

"Grace, I know how important your faith is to you. I'd never ask you to go against it."

"The Bible says that God is love. But those who aren't saved don't have God living inside them because they haven't accepted Jesus as their Savior. Since they don't have God inside their hearts, and God *is* love, how can they love as God meant for them to? Sam, remember when I said that if my mother was still alive, she would've come here with my dad?"

"I remember."

"She had every confidence that my dad would never have made a decision without consulting God about it, without making absolutely sure that it was God's will, and she would have prayed about it and trusted that my dad was doing the right thing. That's what it means to be equally yoked together. It means that both husband and wife are working side by side together to do God's will. But if you have a couple that is unequally yoked, the Christian is strong and trusting in God, always wanting to go the way God wants them to go. But the unbeliever has no relationship with God, and so they make decisions based upon themselves instead of what God wants. And sooner or later, as the Christian continues to obey God, the unbeliever will wander off of the path, wanting to go the way they think is best for them. Then, one of two things will happen, and neither of them is good. Either the unbeliever will leave the Christian, who refuses to disobey God's will and then who must continue on God's path alone without their other half, or the unbeliever will cause the Christian to stray from God's path and completely leave the will of God."

"Grace, I told you, I'd never want you to go against your faith. I may not understand it, but I know how important it is to you."

"Sam, God has commanded me, as a Christian, to not be unequally yoked together with you, a non-Christian. If I start dating you, I will be going against that command, which would put me out of the will of God. Listen to me; I *know* that you don't want me to go against my faith, that you respect what I believe even though you don't understand it. I also know that you want what's best for me because you love me, as I do for you, but even without realizing it, you've already tempted me to disobey God. And it wasn't because you wished to do me evil or that you were purposefully trying to get me to sin, but because it was clear to you that it was simply the next step to take in our relationship."

"I see now what you mean," he said, but it didn't make him feel any better. "Grace, I can't get saved just to be with you. That would be dishonest."

"I wouldn't want you to, Sam. I want you to be saved but for the right reasons. If you did it for me, you'd just be going through the motions and it wouldn't be true salvation. I would know the difference, and more importantly, God would know, too."

"This is why you insisted on calling me Dr. Gray instead of Sam," he finally realized. "To try to keep distance between us."

"Yes," she confirmed, her eyes full of sadness.

"So we love each other but we can't date each other. What exactly are we supposed to do now?" he asked her, frustrated at the whole situation. "I can't . . . I can't just walk away from you, Grace. Not now that I know you feel the same way about me as I do about you."

"I don't want you to, Sam."

"Then what do we do?"

"Well, for starters, you could tell Dr. Williamson that you won't need him to come to the school anymore," Grace said and smiled when she heard him laugh. *I missed that laugh*, she thought to herself.

"I'd already planned to do that," Sam told her. He looked into her eyes, and a serious expression came over him. "Grace, you could have just let me go, thinking you didn't care, thinking you wanted nothing to do with me. Why did you take the time to explain what you meant? Why did you tell me that you love me?"

"I didn't want to be the reason you were hurting, Sam. I couldn't let you believe a lie."

"You could have explained without telling me you love me. Why did you do that?"

Grace smiled softly and answered him in a tender voice. "'Open rebuke is better than secret love.'"

Sam smiled at her answer and asked, "And where is that verse found?"

"Proverbs 27:5," she responded.

"I like that verse," he said and saw her smile.

"Me, too," she agreed. "Sam?"

"Yes?"

"Do your friends really think I led you on and then broke your heart?" Grace asked him.

"What? What makes you think that?"

"That's what Dr. Williamson said. He didn't know who I was, and he blamed your lack of sleep on Miss Cloverdale. Not the chatterbox but the stodgy one." Grace saw Sam's face redden and his eyes darken and knew he was angry.

"He actually called you that?" Sam asked in indignation.

"Dr. Williamson said that everyone here calls me that to distinguish me from Esther."

"Not in front of *me* they don't," Sam growled.

"Sam, it doesn't matter what they call me. Do they really think that I was cruel to you?"

"Honestly, I don't know what they think, but whatever it is they think, they don't think it because of anything that I told them because I didn't talk about it."

"Which means that whatever they're thinking, it's nothing but assumptions," Grace concluded. She paused thoughtfully and studied his face as she had when she'd first arrived at the tent. She could see that he appeared much more relaxed, but still, he looked like he hadn't slept in ages. "Sam, when was the last time you got any sleep?"

"Last night," he answered. "Why?"

"I mean good, restful sleep."

"The night before I met your father," he answered and saw her frown.

"But that was almost five weeks ago!" Grace exclaimed.

"And I am painfully aware of that fact, too."

"Why haven't you been sleeping? You'll make yourself sick!"

"I'll be fine; don't worry about me," he said dismissively.

"Seriously, Sam, lack of sleep for any amount of time is not healthy, and you, of all people, should understand that. What's going on?"

Sam was tempted to tell her what he'd been enduring on a nightly basis, knowing that she wouldn't think him crazy or make fun of him; but still, something kept him from doing it. "I think it's probably that I'm just not used to sleeping in the borrowed bed in a strange place."

For some odd reason, Grace could sense that he was holding something back, although she couldn't tell what it could possibly be. "I'll pray that the Lord will give you some good sleep," she said. "Oh! That reminds me, I wanted to ask you something."

"What?"

"If you aren't working, I'd like it if you'd come to church this Sunday." She watched him shift from one foot to the other and knew she'd made him uncomfortable.

"I'm no longer working on Sundays, but I . . . "

"I understand," Grace said when his words trailed off. "It's a shame you'll miss hearing me sing."

"You sing in front of the church?" he asked her.

"Yes, and I'm in the choir, too," she answered.

"I'd like to hear you sing," Sam said.

Grace smiled and replied, "Come Sunday morning and you will."

Sam studied her face and saw hope still in her eyes. He remembered the last time she'd invited him to church and remembered vividly how disappointed she'd been and how awful he'd felt when the hope in her eyes had died. "I'll be there," he said softly and felt his heart race when the resulting smile lit up her entire face, her skin seeming to radiate light.

"You will? You really will?" she asked.

"I promise," he vowed, and he meant it.

* * *

Sunday morning, Sam was wearing a white dress shirt, black suit jacket, pants, tie, socks, and dress shoes, as ready as he was going to get for church. Picking up his truck keys from the little table near the front door, he then placed his hand on the doorknob to open it. He was surprised when suddenly he heard someone knocking. Opening the door, he found an African woman holding a very young child, and the woman was very distraught.

"Doctor?" she asked in Swahili.

"Yes," he answered.

"Please help me! He's not breathing!"

Sam shoved his keys in his pocket and then took the boy from his mother's arms. "Come inside," he said to her and then set the boy on the couch to examine him.

* * *

"You look especially nice today, sis," Esther said as she stood beside Grace and their father in the little lobby of the church. "You ready to sing?"

Grace was biting her bottom lip and twirling a strand of hair as she stared at the door, praying that Sam would keep his promise that he would come today.

"Hey, Grace, do you hear me?" Esther prodded. When Grace said nothing, Esther glanced at her father.

Thomas put an arm around his distracted daughter, knowing who she was looking for. "Grace, honey, church is about to start."

"He'll be here; I know he will," Grace said firmly.

"Honey, you know how Satan works," Thomas said gently. "He'll give Sam every reason not to come, and because Sam isn't saved, it'll be his nature to listen."

"I know, but he *promised* me, Dad," Grace said.

"We can't wait any longer, Grace," Thomas said.

Disappointment in her eyes, she forced herself not to cry as she walked into the auditorium with her father and sister. *He promised me,* she thought to herself and wiped a stray tear from her eye.

* * *

Sam pulled into the church parking lot, hoping he was not late, and was disheartened to see people leaving the building to go home. He got out of his truck, hoping that she was still there, and began to walk toward the entrance when he noticed her seated on the edge of the concrete slab that led up to the church steps, her right foot absently pushing around a little gray stone in the dirt at her feet. He could tell she was upset, and it wasn't hard for him to figure out why. He hoped she would listen to his explanation.

Grace was staring at the little stone she was moving around with her foot when a pair of black dress shoes came into view. Raising her head, she saw Sam standing in front of her, wearing a suit and tie, looking all ready for church.

"I'm sorry; I tried to get here as fast as I could. I was just about to leave the house when someone knocked on my door. When I opened it, there was an African woman holding her two-year-old son. She told me he wasn't breathing and begged me for help. I examined him and found that he had a roach lodged in the back of his throat. I couldn't get it with my fingers—it was too far down for that—so I had to do a lot of improvising, and I had to do an emergency tracheotomy with a kitchen knife and an ink pen. Poor kid, I couldn't even anesthetize him. Took me twenty minutes to get that bug out of his throat; then I had to remove the makeshift trach tube and treat the hole I'd had to make in his throat, which took me another fifteen minutes. As soon as I could, I jumped in the truck and drove straight here."

"Did the boy live?" Grace asked quietly.

"Yes, he did. Another couple of minutes and he would've suffocated, though. It was way too close. I really am sorry that I missed it, Grace."

"It's all right, Sam. I'd have done the same if I'd been in your situation. I'm glad the boy is okay."

Sam watched her foot push the stone around for a few more minutes, and then he moved to sit down, making sure to sit out of arms' length of her, knowing it's what she would want. "What did you sing?"

"'The Old Rugged Cross,'" she answered. "It's one of my favorites, and it went well with Dad's sermon."

"I would've liked to have heard you sing it," Sam said. After a brief pause, Sam heard the first lines of the song, and he looked over at her to stare in wonder as the most angelic voice he'd ever heard came from her throat and out through her lips to fill the air around them. As he listened to her sing the old hymn, he felt an odd sensation, almost like a tugging on his heart. Even after she had finished with the song, that tugging did not go away, and he thought of asking her about it; but he decided it would go away eventually, and so he said nothing.

* * *

That night, Grace prayed for all of those on her prayer list, read her four chapters in her Bible, and then went to bed, her thoughts on Sam and how he'd promised to come to church this coming Sunday. She prayed that next time nothing would hinder him from being there.

* * *

Sam crawled into bed, lay down, and covered up, feeling worn and weary but happy that he'd gotten to spend at least part of the day with Grace. As he did every night, he hoped he'd get a good night's sleep, and although he had been getting a little more sleep than before since Grace had told him she'd pray for him, he still wasn't sleeping through the night. Tonight was no different, for as soon as he closed his eyes, he could see her face, the strange sadness in her eyes.

"For the wages of sin is death, Sam. If you died today, do you know where you would spend eternity, Sam? You wouldn't go to Heaven; you'd go to Hell, Sam. Because you aren't saved, Sam. For the wages of sin is death, Sam. If you died today, do you know where you would spend eternity, Sam? You wouldn't go to Heaven; you'd go to Hell, Sam. Because you aren't saved, Sam. For the wages of sin is . . . "

CHAPTER SIX

*"And he said unto me, My grace is sufficient for thee: for my strength
is made perfect in weakness. Most gladly therefore will I rather glory
in my infirmities, that the power of Christ may rest upon me."*

2 Corinthians 12:9

EARLY THE NEXT MORNING, GRACE got up, put a robe on, and went to the bathroom. She then went to the closet and pulled out a towel, setting it aside, then turned the water on, adjusting the temperature until it was how she wanted it. Pulling the shower curtain closed, she pulled the knob that switched the water from the faucet to the showerhead, and then she began to undress. Once undressed, she got into the shower and washed her hair, humming to herself, looking forward to starting the school day. When her hair was clean, she began scrubbing her body, but when she got to her chest, she frowned. Looking down, she pressed in a few places and felt a wave of fear go through her when her fingertips detected the small lump that should not have been there. Pressing more firmly on it, she realized it was wider than she'd first thought. *Lord, please don't let this be what I think it is*, she prayed to herself.

* * *

Esther was in the living room fixing her hair when Grace came from down the hall. Esther glanced at her sister and then back to the little decorative mirror on the wall. "Mornin,' sis," Esther said conversationally, not seeing her sister's too-pale face and fright-filled eyes.

"Esther, can you take my class? Something's come up, and I've got to see about it."

"Sure I can, but what's going on?"

"I'd rather not say right now. I don't know how long I'll be but I'll be back as soon as I can."

"Okay, sis. I'll see you at school when you get back." If Esther had been looking at her sister, she would've instantly known that something was very wrong just by seeing that Grace's hair was still wet from the shower, for Grace never went anywhere with her hair in disarray.

* * *

"Miss Cloverdale, how are you today?" Laura asked when she saw Grace walk up to the sign-in table.

"I'm doing well," Grace said automatically and picked up the clipboard and a pen from the table.

"If you need to see a doctor, Sam is taking adults today. One of our general practitioners is out sick, so Sam is picking up the slack for him. He's not busy right now either, so I could go get him if—"

"No, don't," Grace said. "Is there a female doctor available?"

Laura looked at Grace's face and realized that something wasn't right; but it wasn't her business to pry, and so she said nothing. "Dr. Jackson is available. I'm pretty sure she can see you now."

"That will be fine," Grace said. On the clipboard, she wrote "Grace Cloverdale—sick visit." She handed it back to the nurse and said, "I'd appreciate it if you didn't mention this to Sam."

"I won't say a word, Miss Cloverdale," Laura promised. "I'll go get Dr. Jackson and be right back."

"Thank you," Grace said gratefully.

"You're welcome. Oh, by the way, did you know that Sam's birthday is coming up?"

Grace smiled and shook her head. "No, he didn't tell me. When is it?"

"This Thursday," Laura answered.

"Thank you for letting me know," Grace said and then went to sit down.

Not long after Laura had gone, she came back and sat down. Right then right after she'd returned, Dr. Tanya Jackson walked into the waiting room.

"You said I have a patient?" Tanya asked Laura and received the clipboard from the nurse. Tanya looked toward the chairs and called out, "Gra—" Tanya frowned, looked back down at the clipboard, saw that what she'd read was right, and her jaw clenched, her body stiffening. "Grace Cloverdale," she called and watched as the missionary's daughter stood up and walked over to her.

"Good morning, Dr. Jackson," Grace said kindly, knowing full well that the female doctor did not like her.

"Follow me," was all Tanya said.

Grace followed the black-haired woman into a room similar to the one Sam had taken her to the day before. She sat down in the folding chair and waited for the question she knew would come.

"So what seems to be the problem?" Tanya asked.

In Grace's no-nonsense way, she got right to the point. "This morning, I found a lump in my left breast."

Tanya's eyes went wide with shock, but she forced herself to calm down again. "Well, it could just be a benign cyst. If it is, it will eventually go away on its own, and there would be no danger. I'll have to call the hospital and get you scheduled for a mammogram and a biopsy to confirm the diagnosis."

"How soon can all of that be done?" Grace asked.

"Well, that depends on how busy they are. But let me go make the call and see if they can set it up for today, if possible. Would that work?"

"Yes, please," Grace said. "And Dr. Jackson?"

"Yes?"

"Please don't mention this to Sam. I don't want him worrying over nothing."

Tanya was offended at the mere suggestion that she would violate doctor-patient privacy laws. "Miss Cloverdale, you are my patient. It would be against the law to discuss this with anyone but you, and I am offen—"

"I know, but promise me you won't tell him."

"Miss Cloverdale—"

"*Promise me,*" Grace said firmly.

"Very well, I promise," Tanya said through clenched teeth. "I'll go make the phone call."

* * *

Sam parked his truck in front of the school, grabbed his medical bag, and he and Laura exited the vehicle. Immediately, he heard sounds of children laughing and playing, which was odd since it was still time for Bible lessons, and he knew it wasn't even close to recess time. Shrugging it off, he opened one of the double doors and walked in to see Adisa coming out of the girl's restroom halfway down the hall. Instead of turning to her classroom, she turned toward Sam. "Hey, Adisa, why aren't you in class?" Sam asked the girl.

"Miss Cloverdale excused us from our lessons for the day, but we couldn't go home because she knew you would be coming to check up on us, so she sent us out to play and wait for you," the girl answered readily.

"What about the other classes?" Sam asked.

"It's just ours, Dr. Gray. The others are still having class."

"Okay, well I'll be right out in a few minutes to check on you. Nurse Laura here can go with you and start the basic stuff."

"Okay," she said. She was about to go outside when she paused and turned back to the doctor. "Dr. Gray?"

"Yes?"

"I think . . . I think something's wrong with Miss Cloverdale," Adisa said hesitantly.

Sam frowned and asked, "Why do you think that?"

"She's been staring off into space all morning, and her eyes look kinda red, like she's been crying. Did you have another fight with her?"

Sam's frown deepened, and he answered, "No, I didn't. You go on out with Nurse Laura, and I'll go check on Miss Cloverdale."

"Okay," Adisa said, relieved, and then left with the nurse.

Sam hurried to the classroom, and instead of knocking on the closed door, he went ahead and opened it. He walked in and saw Grace seated at her teacher's desk, her eyes staring out the window.

As soon as he saw that she was wearing bright colors—a short-sleeved yellow dress shirt with green ivy and orange flowers on it, a tea-length orange pencil skirt, and white sandals—Sam knew something was wrong. The only times he'd seen her wear bright colors was when Esther had chosen to wash all of Grace's clothes, even the clean ones, which forced Grace to borrow some of Esther's, and when Mshindi had died. Looking at her too-pale face and reddened eyes, Sam didn't think it was because of laundry. He debated closing the door to give them privacy but he knew she wouldn't approve; and so instead, he walked over to one of the front desks and pulled it over to the teacher's desk beside her chair then sat in it. "Good morning, Grace," he said softly.

Grace turned to look at him and gave him a welcoming smile, but it faded quickly. "Good morning, Sam," she said.

"Been daydreaming too much and the kids mutinied, I think," he said and smiled when she laughed, but the laughter rang hollow and died too quickly. *Something is very wrong*, he thought.

"No, I dismissed school for the day. I did make them stay close to the school because I knew you'd be here to give them their checkups." Grace looked past him and then back at him. "Where's Laura? Didn't she come with you?"

"She did. I ran into Adisa in the hallway, and she explained where the kids are and why. I sent Laura to start their checkups."

"Well, I'm glad you came in here. I have something for you."

"You do?" Sam questioned and watched her open up the top right drawer and take something out. When she turned around, she was holding out a burgundy-wrapped box that had a gold ribbon wrapped around it and tied on the top.

"I know it's a day late, but happy birthday, Sam," she declared, smiling.

"How did you know?"

"I have my ways," she said mysteriously. "Go on; open it."

Sam began to untie the gold ribbon, curious as to what it could be.

"I didn't know what to get you at first, but then I got to thinking about it, and it suddenly came to me."

"What is it?" he asked as he set aside the ribbon and moved to open the box top.

"I got you the one thing that everyone needs but that I knew you didn't have," Grace said and watched his face.

The instant Sam saw the words "Holy Bible," he knew he should've expected it, though he didn't know why he hadn't. "Well, you're right," he said as he lifted the Bible out of the box, noticing that "Dr. Sam M. Gray" had been printed at the bottom right corner in gold lettering. "I definitely didn't have one."

"I figured you could bring it with you to church this Sunday, since I know you plan to come. You'll be able to follow along when Dad reads the Scriptures."

"That's a good idea. I never thought about needing a Bible for church. Thank you, Grace."

"You really like it?"

"Of course I do," he said, and he meant it. His heart warmed when she smiled that big smile that made her face glow and her eyes light up.

"Here, let me show you something," she said and opened the Bible to the third page.

Sam looked at the page and smiled. At the top of the page, it said "Presented" and below that it said "To Dr. Sam M. Gray." On the second line, it said "By Miss Grace S. Cloverdale" and on the third and final line, it said "On May 12th, 1993." He looked back up into her eyes and was about to say something, but she spoke up before he could.

"Wait, there's something else, too," she said and then turned back to the first page, which should have been blank.

Sam looked down and saw she had written something there, and so silently, he began to read it.

My Beloved Sam,

I want you to know that I love you more than any words could ever express and that I will love you forever, no matter what may come. There are two verses I want you to remember. In John 5:24, Jesus said 'Verily, verily, I say unto you, He that heareth my word, and believeth on him that sent me, hath everlasting life, and shall not come into condemnation; but is passed from death unto life.' The second verse is one of my favorites, and it is Romans 8:28. 'And we know that all things work together for good to them that love God, to them who are the called according to his purpose.' Don't forget them, Sam.

With All My Love,

Grace S. Cloverdale

Sam smiled at her and said tenderly, "I love you, too, Grace." He turned the pages, passing the page she'd shown him before, passing the page for marriage, children's births and marriages, and was about to pass the one for deaths when he caught sight of more handwriting. Frowning, he looked at the top line, which had been filled out. It said "Grace S. Cloverdale: September 20, 1970-January ?, 1994."

Silently, Grace watched him read what she had written, praying silently for him.

Sam tapped the date of death and said, "Grace, that's not very funny."

"It isn't meant to be funny, Sam." Her tone was calm and quiet.

"I don't understand. Why would you put that in here?"

Grace covered his hand with hers and looked him in the eyes. "That's how long the doctors have given me."

"What? What are you talking about? Seriously, Grace, this is *not* funny!"

"Sam, I need you to remain calm for me, please."

"Tell me what's going on, Grace!"

"I have breast cancer," she said as gently as she could.

"Breast cancer can be treated," said the doctor automatically, "and removed if need be. If worse comes to worse, a mastectomy can be performed. It's not a death sentence like it used to be. I—"

"Mine is too deep, Sam, and too aggressive. Treatment won't work, and because of its location, surgery isn't an option. There's nothing that can be done."

Sam got to his feet and began to pace, his mind racing, unwilling to believe what she was saying. "You could get a second opinion. Maybe the first doctor was wrong. Maybe the test results got mixed—"

"Sam, two doctors have already looked at the tests, and everything has been confirmed," she said, watching him pacing back and forth, hearing the desperation in his voice.

"They have to be wrong! They *have* to be!" he shouted angrily.

"Dr. Gray," she said, and she saw him freeze to look at her, "they aren't wrong."

"I refuse to accept that!"

Calmly, Grace opened up one of her desk drawers, took out a large manila envelope, stood up, and walked over to where he was. "See for yourself," she said and handed the envelope to him. In silence, she watched as he opened it and read the results of the biopsy for himself, saw the film of the mammogram they had enclosed for her, and read the apologetic letter notifying her that the lump was inoperable and that, based upon the aggressive nature of the cancer, she had an estimated eight months to live. When he'd looked at everything in the envelope and had raised his eyes to look at her, she gently took the documents from his hands and began putting them back into the envelope. When she looked back up at his face, the stricken look in his eyes nearly broke her heart.

"Why?" he whispered then. "Why you?"

"'I have fought a good fight, I have finished my course, I have kept the faith,' 2 Timothy 4:7," she answered him softly.

Sam stared into her calm, beautiful eyes and felt anger boiling up inside him suddenly. "It isn't fair," he said.

"'Jesus said unto her, I am the resurrection and the life: he that believeth in me, though he were dead, yet shall he live,' John 11:25. And I believe in Him, Sam," she told him.

"How could He do this to you, Grace? You've done everything He wanted, you've obeyed Him in everything; you even refused a relationship with me even though you wanted one; and *this* is how He repays you?"

"'Precious in the sight of the Lord is the death of his saints,' Psalm 116:15," was her answer.

"What about me, Grace?" he asked her. "While you're up there in Heaven, I'll be stuck down here with—*without you!*"

"'Blessed are they that mourn: for they shall be comforted,' Matthew 5:4," she quoted, knowing he would recall the verse from when Mshindi had died.

Grabbing her roughly by her shoulders, he looked into her eyes and said, "How can you be so *calm* about this?!"

"Jesus said 'Peace I leave with you, my peace I give unto you: not as the world giveth, give I unto you. Let not your heart be troubled, neither let it be afraid.' That's John 14:27."

"So you aren't afraid, not at all?!"

Grace smiled at him sadly and said, "Of course I am afraid. Even Jesus was afraid to die."

That surprised him, for he'd never heard that before. "He . . . He *was?*"

"'Then saith he unto them, My soul is exceeding sorrowful, even unto death: tarry ye here, and watch with me. And he went a little further, and fell on his face, and prayed, saying, O my Father, if it be possible, let this cup pass from me: nevertheless not as I will, but as thou wilt.' That's Matthew 26:38-39. He knew He was about to be crucified; He even knew exactly what He would have to endure, and He was afraid. Most people forget that although Jesus was God, He was also man, too. He didn't want to die; He even prayed to God that if it was at all possible that He not die. But He also was willing to do what God wanted Him to, and through prayer, God gave Jesus the strength to endure the cross."

"Grace, I don't . . . I don't want you to die," he whispered and felt tears stinging his eyes.

"And I don't want to die," she said quietly, her shoulders shaking. "I'm afraid of what it will feel like and of whether it will hurt or not.

And I don't want to leave you behind to face this alone. If you were saved, I'd know you'd have God to help you through, but I don't even have that as comfort. But listen to me, Sam; don't worry for me. I have eternal life, remember?"

Sam pulled her against him and held her tightly, hiding his face in her long hair, the pain in his heart so sharp and cutting that he couldn't bear it. "He can't take you from me, Grace; He *can't!*"

"He is God, Sam; He can do what He wants," she said gently and closed her eyes when he heard him begin to sob as he held her, knowing there was really nothing she could say to help him through this.

"This isn't fair," he said again as he cried into her hair. "I love you, Grace; I love you *so* much."

"I know you do, Sam," she said tenderly to him. "I love you, too."

"It just isn't fair . . . "

* * *

That night when Grace took out her prayer list, she wrote her name at the top of the "Illness" section and then began praying for everyone on her list, beginning with the unsaved as she always did. This night, needing the extra comfort and not wanting to go to sleep yet, she read an extra four chapters of her Bible in addition to the four she would normally have read. When she began to feel sleepy, she got into bed, lay down, and covered up. Before she went to sleep, she prayed. "Lord, I know that You will see me through this; I know that everything always works together for good to those who love You. If it is Your will, let this cancer go away. But if it is Your will that I should endure it, give me the comfort and peace that only You can provide; help me to remain strong. And, Lord, if my course truly is finished, I beg You for one more thing. Before You call me home to Heaven, I want more than anything else to see Sam accept Jesus as his Savior. He's going to need You now more than ever. Please, God, let me see him saved before I die. In Jesus' name, I pray, amen." She fell asleep with peace in her heart and tears on her cheeks.

* * *

Sam sat on his bed staring at the Bible that Grace had given to him for his birthday as though it was a snake about to bite him. "I don't understand," he said to the Book. "She's given her life to You, done everything You've asked—and gladly—but You're just going to kill her. I thought You were supposed to be merciful."

"*'Precious in the sight of the Lord is the death of his saints,' Psalm 116:15,*" he heard her say again.

"This isn't fair, God! Not to *her*!" he shouted at the Book angrily.

"*'Jesus said unto her, I am the resurrection and the life: he that believeth in me, though he were dead, yet shall he live,' John 11:25,*" her voice came again into his head.

"I can't live without her; I don't *want* to live without her. I love her," Sam said miserably and felt tears falling from his face again.

"*'Blessed are they that mourn: for they shall be comforted,' Matthew 5:4,*" said Grace in his mind.

"I don't *want* to be comforted! I want *her*!" he yelled. Furiously wiping the tears from his eyes, he grabbed the Bible and glared at it. Taking it in both hands, he opened it up and read the first verse he saw. The hairs on the back of his neck stood up when he saw the familiar words. "'For the wages of sin is death; but the gift of God is eternal life through Jesus Christ our Lord,'" he read aloud. He shut the Book, feeling the anger seething inside of him and beneath that, the pain of knowing that there was nothing he could do to save Grace. Again he opened up the Bible and again he read the first verse he saw. Again, he felt the hairs on the back of his neck stand up. "'But God commendeth his love toward us, in that, while we were yet sinners, Christ died for us.'" Shutting the Bible a second time, he took a deep breath, ignoring the fresh tears in his eyes, and opened the Book one final time. "'For whosoever shall call upon the name of the Lord shall be saved,'" he read the verse.

"If this is what You do to those who love You and follow You, why would I want to be saved?" he asked as he stared at the Book.

Once again, Grace's voice rang inside his head, so calm and strong. *"Jesus said 'Peace I leave with you, my peace I give unto you: not as the world giveth, give I unto you. Let not your heart be troubled, neither let it be afraid.' That's John 14:27."*

Closing the Bible, he set it on the nearby nightstand, got into bed and lay down, covering himself up. His thoughts went back to Grace and how she had stood there so calmly as she'd explained what the doctors had told her. He had seen the fear in her eyes, for there had been no disguising it, but even though she'd been afraid, he could also see that the inner strength she carried with her was still there and he couldn't understand how she could still continue to love God when her life was ending. He knew for certain that this night, he would get no sleep at all; and so when he shut his eyes and saw her sad face in his mind, heard those words that never seemed to leave him now, he wasn't at all surprised.

"For the wages of sin is death, Sam. If you died today, do you know where you would spend eternity, Sam? You wouldn't go to Heaven; you'd go to Hell,

Sam. Because you aren't saved, Sam. But God commendeth his love toward us, in that, while we were yet sinners, Christ died for us. For the wages of sin is death, Sam. If you died today, do you know where you would spend eternity, Sam? You wouldn't go to Heaven; you'd go to Hell, Sam. Because you aren't saved, Sam. But God commendeth his love toward us, in that, while we were yet sinners, Christ died for us. For the wages of sin is . . . "

CHAPTER SEVEN

"For the grace of God that bringeth salvation hath appeared to all men."

Titus 2:11

THE NEXT AFTERNOON, SAM WALKED into the little house he was staying at and rubbed his tired eyes. Not really hungry, he went to the fridge mostly out of habit and looked to see what he had to eat, but his mind was so preoccupied with thoughts of Grace that he didn't really see anything. He was reaching for a container of leftover rice when he heard the wall phone begin to ring. Shutting the fridge, he went over to the wall phone and lifted the receiver up, hoping it wasn't more bad news. "Dr. Sam Gray," he answered as he always did in case it was someone trying to reach him for business reasons.

"Good afternoon, Sam; it's Dr. Cloverdale," Thomas' voice came over the line. "I hope I'm not disturbing you."

"You aren't," Sam said. "I just got home, as a matter of fact. Is something wrong? One of the kids aren't sick, are they?"

* * *

"No, the children are all fine," Thomas assured the doctor, frowning at the man's response. Thomas could hear the weariness in the younger man's voice, and having been told by Grace that Sam

127

hadn't been sleeping at all, the missionary could only imagine what kind of stress Grace's news had heaped upon the already-disturbed doctor. Sam's next response only confirmed Thomas' belief.

"It's not Grace, is it? She—"

"No, Sam, everyone is all right. There is no emergency," Thomas said and felt sorry for the young man.

"Good," Sam said, sighing with relief as he ran a nervous hand through his hair. "That's good."

Grace is right, Thomas thought to himself. *He needs cheering up.* "The reason why I'm calling is that I was wondering if you'd like to come over for a visit and stay for dinner tonight."

Sam blinked, thinking he'd misheard. "Tonight?"

"Yes, unless you're busy."

"N-no, I'm not busy."

"I'm glad to hear it. Do you like to play board games?"

"Board games?"

"Yes, like *Sorry!* and *Monopoly* . . . board games."

"Well, I did when I was a kid, but it's been a long time since I've played any," Sam said, finding the conversation surreal.

"Then I feel it only fair to warn you that as soon as you come in, Esther will bother you to play board games with her."

"*Dad!*" came a familiar voice in the background over the line.

Sam chuckled when he heard Esther's voice. "I think I could stand to play a few games," Sam said graciously.

"She'll be ecstatic," Thomas said.

"What's for dinner?" Sam asked curiously.

"Just a second," Thomas said. Then, away from the receiver, he yelled, "Grace, honey, Sam wants to know what you're making for dinner!"

"Tell him it's a surprise and that if he wants to know, he'll have to come over and find out!" Grace responded.

Thomas put the phone back up to his ear and asked, "Did you hear that?"

Laughing heartily, Sam answered, "I heard. What time should I be over?"

"Dinner won't be ready until around six, but you can come over now if you want."

"Let me get cleaned up and change clothes, and then I'll be over, probably in about an hour or so."

"That'll be fine, Sam. See you then," Thomas said.

"See you," Sam said and hung up the phone. Then he went to go take a quick shower.

* * *

"Is he coming?" Grace asked, coming out of the kitchen.

"He'll be here in about an hour. You were right, Grace; he sounds . . ." Thomas searched for the right word, but it was Grace who found it.

"Defeated," she supplied, her voice sad.

"Yes," Thomas nodded. "I think this will be good for him. When I called, he immediately thought that something had happened to one of the children, and then when I told him that the kids were fine, he was afraid it was about you."

"He doesn't know how to handle this," Grace said. "And the lack of sleep is just making things worse. I asked him why he hasn't been sleeping, but all he said was that he thinks it's because he's just not used to sleeping in a strange house. I know it's more than that, though. When he comes, pay attention to his face. You'll see what I mean."

"Poor Sam," Esther said sadly. "I wish there was something else we could do besides pray for him and give him a fun night. Oh, what did he say about the board games?"

"He said he'd be happy to play with you," Thomas said and smiled when Esther gave a whoop of delight. "Listen, Esther, I don't want you to monopolize his time while he's here, do you understand me?"

Esther giggled and said, "Monopolize!"

"I mean it, young lady. He isn't just here to see you, ya know," Thomas reminded her.

"I know," Esther said. "That's why I'm gonna set up the game in the kitchen. Grace will be cooking, and if we play in the living room, he won't be able to visit with her much or she with him."

"Thanks, Esther," Grace said, smiling at her sister.

"No problem! Now, Grace, if you want to freshen up before he gets here, I'll watch the food."

"Okay, but don't you *dare* burn it!"

"Perish the thought, sis. Perish the thought."

* * *

Sam rang the doorbell, and it wasn't too long before the door opened and Esther's grinning face was staring back at him.

"Sam, I'm so happy you could come over! Come on in!" Esther said merrily and forced the grin to remain on her face when she saw how awful he looked, just as Grace had said. *Poor, poor Sam*, she thought to herself. *Please, God, don't let me cry until after he's gone.*

"Thanks for inviting me over. I appreciate it," Sam said and walked in when she moved to let him inside. "Oh, my goodness, what is that wonderful smell?"

"That's dinner, and no, I can't tell you what it is, or Grace will kill me."

"My Grace wouldn't hurt a fly," Sam said instantly and then noticed Dr. Cloverdale moving to stand. His face reddened when he realized he'd called her *his* Grace. "Um, that is . . ."

"I hate to tell you this, but your Grace has killed plenty of flies," Thomas said good-naturedly and held out his hand to Sam, inwardly concerned for the young doctor when he saw the younger man's weary eyes and haggard features.

Sam laughed and shook the missionary's hand. "Thank you for inviting me, Dr. Cloverdale."

"We're glad to have you, m'boy." Thomas smiled when he saw Sam's eyes search, knowing for whom he was searching.

"Sam, I already set up the board game. Dad says no Monopoly because it's too long, so I set up Sorry! first. I figure if we get tired of playing, we can always switch to something else. We've got plenty to choose from. And I set it up in the kitchen so we can all visit together, since Grace is in there cooking," Esther said.

"I'll follow you then," Sam said. He followed Esther into the kitchen and grinned when he heard her announcement.

"Hey, Grace, look who I've brought with me," she said.

Grace covered the big pot on the stove and then turned, smiling when she saw Sam dressed in a loose-fitting blue t-shirt and relaxed fit blue jeans, gray sneakers on his feet. The t-shirt did nothing to hide his wide shoulders and muscular arms, and she felt her face blush at the sight. "'His mouth is most sweet: yeah, he is altogether lovely. This is my beloved, and this is my friend, O daughters of Jerusalem,'" she said by way of welcoming him and watched him smile.

"Let me guess," Sam said, "Song of Solomon?"

"'The voice of my beloved! behold, he cometh leaping upon the mountains, skipping upon the hills,'" she exclaimed, her eyes shining with undisguised joy.

"You look beautiful, Grace," he said softly to her and watched her blush deepen.

She wore a dress the same shade as her eyes,;her feet were bare; and her beautiful hair had been left to flow down her shoulders and back, save for what had been braided and coiled atop her head like a crown.

"If I knew any verses that could describe how beautiful you look, I'd quote them," Sam said. He felt a tug on his arm, and then Esther was whispering into his ear. "Wow, that's a good one, Esther." Grinning, he then looked at Grace and said, "'As the lily among thorns, so is my love among the daughters.'"

Grace put her hand up to her mouth and giggled. "Song of Solomon 2:2," she said knowingly.

"I've got another one, Sam," Esther said and whispered the verse into his ear.

"'Who is she that looketh forth as the morning, fair as the moon, clear as the sun,'" Sam said and saw Grace's face turn deep red.

"Song of Solomon 6:10a," she said, fully embarrassed now. "Let's start the game so that my face can recover."

"What color do you want to be, Sam?" Esther asked.

"Ladies go first." Sam grinned.

"No, no, you're our guest. You pick," Esther said.

"Anything but red," Sam answered then.

"You don't like red?" Esther queried.

"I like it just fine. But it's Grace's favorite color," he said and saw Grace's eyes give him a loving look for his answer.

"All right, Grace gets red," Esther said, turning the board so that the red would be closest to where Grace was. "I want the yellow, if no one objects."

"Then I'll take blue," Sam said.

"I guess that leaves me with the green," Thomas said.

When they were all seated in their respective places, except for Grace who was watching the food cooking in the pot on the stove, Thomas shuffled the cards and had everyone draw a card to see who went first. Esther won, and then Thomas shuffled the cards again and put them down on the "Face Down" rectangle. "Let the game begin," he declared with a grin, eliciting laughter from everyone else.

* * *

"I suspect that Colonel Mustard killed Mr. Boddy in the Conservatory with the candlestick!" Esther declared, many hours and many games later. "Prove me wrong!"

The others shuffled through their Clue cards, searching to see if they could.

"Well, I can't," Sam said.

"Neither can I," Thomas confessed.

"Uh oh, I can't either," Grace said and then set her cards down to go check on the food.

Esther gave an excited whoop and then cleared her throat. "Okay, I *accuse* Colonel Mustard, that dastardly man, of killing Mr. Boddy in the Conservatory with the candlestick!" Esther said. Grinning, she reached for the little card-sized envelope marked "CONFIDENTIAL" across it and opened it up to look inside. "Ha ha, I win!" she exclaimed, putting the cards down so everyone could see.

"That's good," Grace said, "because it's time to set the table for dinner."

"Good because I'm starving," Thomas said and moved to help Esther and Sam put the game up.

When the game had been put away, Esther began setting the table.

"Can I help set the table?" Sam asked.

"You can get some glasses down and put some ice into them," Esther answered as she set out four large soup bowls before going to get four spoons.

By the time Grace pronounced that the food was done, the table had been set, and the others had washed their hands and returned to the kitchen. Grace placed a potholder in the center of the table, put her oven mitts on, and lifted the heavy pot to carry it over to the table, setting it down on the potholder. Removing the oven mitts and setting them aside, she then got a ladle out of a drawer and sat down at the table, standing the ladle up against the large pot. "All right, everyone, time to ask the blessing," she said, and everyone quieted down. "Dad?"

They bowed their heads, and Thomas asked God's blessing over the food and the evening, praying that everyone would continue to have a good time.

"Sam, pass your bowl please," Grace said. When he did, Grace lifted the lid off of the pot and set it aside, took the ladle, and began filling up Sam's bowl. Once it was full, she passed it back to him and then asked for Esther's bowl.

"Homemade chili," Sam said, impressed, and his stomach rumbled in anticipation. "It looks delicious, Grace."

"Thank you," Grace said demurely.

"Trust me, Sam, it *is* delicious," Esther promised as she received her own bowl. "Do you want some crackers?"

"I think I'll try it without first," Sam said.

"Here you go, Dad," Grace said, passing him his bowl before filling her own and then sitting down in her chair. "Dig in, everyone."

Sam tried his chili, and his eyes widened. "Oh, wow, it's *wonderful*," he declared. "Grace, you're an amazing cook."

"Thank you; I'm glad you like it."

They took their time eating dinner, talking and joking and laughing, enjoying each other's company. After they'd all had seconds, Grace put the chili pot back on the stove and covered it up, then opened the oven and took out the two pies she'd made for dessert.

"Esther, can you go get the plates?" Grace asked, setting the pies on the table.

"Sure," Esther said and got up.

"Who wants cherry, and who wants apple?"

"I want one of each," Sam said immediately.

"I think I will have what Sam's having," Thomas said, grinning at the doctor.

"Cherry for me, sis!" Esther called.

"And I want apple," Grace said. "Well, these pies aren't going to last very long, I can tell."

"Whatever made you think they would?" Thomas asked, laughing.

* * *

After dessert, Grace took Sam's arm and excused herself, heading toward the back door with him in tow. Going outside, she led him over to what looked like a handmade porch swing and sat down beside him. "Well, I'm certainly full," she said.

"So am I. You really are a wonderful cook."

"Thank you," she said, smiling shyly as she lazily swung them both. "So which did you like best, the apple or the cherry pie?"

"Apple, by far. The cherry is good, too, but the apple pie is the best I've ever had."

"I like the apple best, too. Are you having fun?"

"Are you kidding? I can't remember when I've had this much fun!"

Grace smiled, hearing the change in his voice, the lack of stress, and knew that this night had been good for him. "I'm glad," she said.

Sam looked at her and reached out to take her right hand in his. "How are you doing?"

"Excited for tomorrow," she answered instantly. "I won't be singing like I was last week, but you'll be there, and that's what matters."

"That's not what I meant," Sam said softly.

"I know what you meant, Sam," she said, "but I'm not going to think about it tonight."

"So how was school today?"

"Eventful," she answered. "Mbwana found a bug and decided he'd bring it into class with him. It got loose and managed to crawl up Lakicia's leg, which of course made her scream, scaring the rest of us. Well, I had no idea what was going on, and all I could do was watch as she stood up and started dancing around the room. Of course, she wasn't dancing—she was trying to get the bug off of her—but I didn't know that at the time . . . "

As Grace continued the story, Sam broke out into laughter, picturing it all in his mind as his eyes watched her animated facial expressions, and for a little while, he forgot about her cancer.

* * *

On Sunday morning, Sam ate some leftover chili for breakfast, having been given some before he'd left the Cloverdale house the night before; and once full, he got dressed. Picking his Bible up off of the couch, he was halfway to the door when someone knocked on it. *Not again,* he thought, annoyed. When he opened his front door, he was surprised to find the African woman from the week before, holding her alert boy in her arms. "Is he sick?"

"No," the woman said. "I just wanted to thank you for saving him last week. You left in such a hurry, I didn't get a chance to."

"Oh, well, you're welcome. I'm glad I could help him. Listen, I don't mean to be rude, but I really have to go."

The young mother looked down at the Book and then looked back at the doctor. "Church?" she asked.

"Yeah," Sam answered, and then a thought popped into his head. "Would you like to come?"

The woman looked down at herself, then back up at him. "I'm not dressed for church."

"Somehow," Sam said, "I don't think they'd mind."

Sam held the door open for the young mother and then walked into the church, his eyes looking over the sparse lobby with the two pews, and frowned when he heard upbeat music coming from inside the auditorium.

"Good morning," said an African man dressed in a suit and tie, a welcoming smile upon his face, "and welcome to Lighthouse Baptist Church."

"The service hasn't started yet, has it?" Sam asked in Swahili.

"Oh, no, sir. The choir has just finished singing and this is the start of our handshake song."

"Your . . . what song?"

"Our handshake song. It gives everyone an opportunity to greet guests and friends. Wait a moment, and I can show you to some seats."

"Oh, okay," Sam said, glad he hadn't missed much. *I wish I'd gotten here earlier, though. Grace is probably thinking I'm going to miss today, too, just like last week. Oh, well, hopefully she'll see I'm here,* he thought to himself.

When the usher opened the auditorium door, Sam and the young mother followed. The usher seated the young mother at the back since she had a small child and she might have to take the child out of the auditorium; then he led Sam up front, seating him on the fourth row pew. "Enjoy the service, sir," the usher said and turned around to walk back to the lobby.

Sam set his Bible on the seat, remaining standing with the rest of the congregation, and he grabbed the song book and tried to find the song they were singing. He gave up after a while and just listened to the words, not knowing what else to do. When that song was finished, the song leader called out another song number, and this time, Sam found it and began to sing along as best he could. After that song was over, the congregation sat down, so he did, too, and then watched as Dr. Cloverdale came up to the microphone.

"This morning, Sister Cheboi was supposed to sing a special, but, unfortunately, she came down sick and was forced to stay home. She called me this morning and asked me if I could find someone to take her place. Well, since it was short notice, I had to find the first person I could. I'm sure none of you will mind, however, for she did such a good job last week," Thomas said in Swahili and then turned, motioning toward someone seated behind the piano.

Sam watched as the African woman playing the piano stood up and switched places, and Sam's eyes instantly lit up when he saw Grace seat herself on the piano bench as the song leader brought over a microphone for her.

* * *

Grace straightened the microphone, putting it where it was comfortable for her, and then placed her fingers over the keys. Praying silently that she could get through the song without crying, she began the soft refrain, taking a deep, cleansing breath. Then she began to sing, her voice soft and tender, putting as much feeling into it as she could. In the first verse, she sang of how Jesus had left His disciples in the garden. As His followers slept, He had prayed that He would not have to bear the agony of the cross but that if it was His Father's will, He would obey. After receiving strength from God, Jesus gave Himself as a Sacrifice.

Sam felt a tugging, and he remembered the conversation he'd had with Grace about how Jesus had not wanted to die—how He had asked God to not let Him die—but had gone on to die anyways, knowing it was what God wanted. Knowing what Grace was going through and remembering the fear he'd seen in her eyes as she'd told him, the song pulled at his heart like nothing else ever had. Grace sang the chorus, lifting her voice to give the words strength and power. As she described how Christ had suffered and died just for her so she could have eternal life, Sam could picture himself in the crowd that day as Jesus was crucified, and the tugging on his heart grew stronger.

Once more softening her voice, Grace began the second verse, explaining how Jesus had been betrayed and sold for silver, how Jesus had not refused when the soldiers had come to take Him, and how He had taken every step because of His love for everyone.

Sam listened to her sing the chorus a second time; and as he stared at the woman he loved, seeing the confidence and passion of her faith upon her face, he finally realized where her calm, inner strength had come from and understood what the verse truly meant about having peace not of the world.

Grace smiled, for the third verse had always been her favorite, and now, with what she was going through, it had a much deeper meaning. Her smile widened as she sang of how millions had chosen to trust Jesus all throughout history and that the Savior of this world had loved her enough to give her a way to be saved and to give her faith to know that He has prepared a place in Heaven just for her. Increasing the volume for the final chorus, singing for all she was worth, tears began to fall; but she knew she would make it to the end. As she reached the last two lines of the song, her voice softened once more, reminding the congregation that if they had been the only ones alive, Jesus would still have chosen to die for each one of them.

Sam saw the tears as she'd come to the end of the song, but he knew they weren't sad tears, for she had the most angelic smile upon her face that he'd ever seen, her skin radiant and her eyes sparkling. When she finished the song, as the congregation clapped appreciatively, he watched her stand up and walk over to the podium, facing the congregation.

"I have an announcement to make," Grace said into the microphone as she stared out at the sea of faces, her vision blurring from the tears that were still falling from her face. "Before I make it, I'd like to quote a Bible verse as kind of a reminder to all of my brothers and sisters in Christ. The verse is John 13:36, and Jesus is speaking to His disciples about His upcoming death on the cross. It says, 'Simon Peter said unto him, Lord, wither goest thou? Jesus answered him, Whither I go, thou canst not follow me now; but thou shalt follow me afterwards.' This past Friday, I was diagnosed with breast cancer. Ordinarily, it can be treated or surgically removed. However, my cancer is in a difficult spot and is particularly aggressive. Treatment won't work, and because of its location, an operation would do no good. My doctors have given me eight months to live." Grace remained silent as all around the congregation, there were shocked gasps, outcries, and whisperings as those she had known for four years received the news. "I know it's a lot to take in, but I also know where I'm headed, and I'm ready. I ask that you pray for me and for my family during this time—and also for my students. Also, keep praying for Dr. Sam Gray to be saved, for he will need God's comfort to see him through this. I'll remain on staff as long as I am physically able to. Don't be sad about this. You should all be jealous that I get to see God before any of you," she said.

The congregation laughed even as they cried, for many of them had been led to Jesus by this woman of faith, and they would miss her sorely when she was gone.

* * *

"So before I turn the pulpit over to my dad, I leave you with this final verse. 'And we know that *all things* work together for good to them that love God, to them who are the called according to his purpose,' Romans 8:28. Not some things, but all things, even this.

God bless you all." Grace then walked off of the platform, down past the piano, and around to slide into her pew, glad she hadn't worn makeup, for the tears that she'd held in check during the singing were now flowing freely from her eyes, and she could not stop them even if she'd wanted to. She sat down in her customary place, not even realizing that Sam was seated directly behind her.

When Sam saw her sit in the pew in front of him, he thought she would see him; but when he saw her weeping, he knew she probably couldn't see much of anything. He thought about tapping her on her shoulder; but as soon as Dr. Cloverdale came to the pulpit, she took up her Bible, lifted her eyes toward her father, and prepared to listen to the sermon. Sam didn't want to distract her and decided to wait until after the service to tell her that he'd been here. Just as she had done, Sam grabbed his Bible and looked up at the missionary man and found Dr. Cloverdale looking right back at him, a smile upon his face.

"Turn in your Bibles to Luke chapter sixteen, beginning in verse nineteen," Thomas said in Swahili, a serious tone in his voice. He'd seen Sam sitting behind Grace; and immediately, he began to pray for the young doctor to be saved, along with anyone else who might be there who was still unsaved.

Sam looked up the page for Luke and eventually found the proper passage. As Dr. Cloverdale began to read, Sam followed along. When Thomas reached verse twenty-two, Sam felt that tugging return, but he also felt a growing fear inside his heart and had no explanation for either feeling. The further into the Scriptures the missionary read, the worse those feelings got.

"'And it came to pass, that the beggar died, and was carried by the angels into Abraham's bosom: the rich man also died, and was buried;

And in hell he lift up his eyes, being in torments, and seeth Abraham afar off, and Lazarus in his bosom. And he cried and said, Father Abraham, have mercy on me, and send Lazarus, that he may dip the tip of his finger in water, and cool my tongue; for I am tormented in this flame. But Abraham said, Son, remember that thou in thy lifetime receivedst thy good things, and likewise Lazarus evil things: but now he is comforted, and thou art tormented. And beside all this, between us and you there is a great gulf fixed: so that they which would pass from hence to you cannot; neither can they pass to us that would come from thence.'" Thomas then looked out at the congregation and began to preach the sermon he had prepared.

Sam listened to every word that was preached as Dr. Cloverdale cited passage after passage of how Hell would be dark, filled with torment and the screams of those being tormented in the flames, and other horrors that would've sent the bravest man screaming in terror. That fear in his heart just kept growing and growing and growing until it was so thick, he was nearly choking on it. At the end of the sermon, the missionary gave what he referred to as the "Invitation" and Sam watched as a lot of people came up to the front and knelt down at the steps that led to the platform, all of them praying. Sam was rooted to his seat, unable to move, paralyzed by the fear that gripped him, his thoughts turning over and over, even when he watched as the young mother he'd brought with him walked up to the front, uncertainty in her bearing. Sam then saw Grace stand to her feet, Bible in hand, and approach the young mother, and then he stared at the two women as Grace led the mother over to the steps. He watched Grace open her Bible and begin to read out of it, speaking to the African woman, flipping a few pages, reading some more, and speaking again. After several more times of that, Sam watched the woman bow her head to pray, and when she'd finished, Grace led her over to the front pew, both women smiling the biggest smiles Sam had ever seen.

Sam felt an inexplicable pull to go up, but something held him back, told him to just stay there until the feeling had gone. So Sam remained where he was, and eventually, the Invitation was closed. Once the music stopped, he heard Dr. Cloverdale introduce the young mother and announce that the woman had accepted Jesus as her Savior. Still, the feeling of fear and the tugging at his heart continued, and when Dr. Cloverdale asked everyone to stand for the dismissal prayer, Sam could not even rise to his feet. In shock, his mind replaying the sermon he'd just heard; Sam watched as what seemed like the entire congregation lined up and shook the young mother's hand before speaking with Grace—most of them crying.

Nearly an hour later, the auditorium had emptied out, and Grace stood to gather her things. But she caught sight of the piano; so, instead of going to the pew where her purse still sat, she carried her Bible over to the piano, set the precious Book beside her on the bench, and positioned her fingers over the keys.

Sam watched as Grace's hands shook, worry crossing over her features; but then as he continued to stare at her, he saw her back straighten, her head lift up, her eyes close, and a smile slowly spread upon her face, drawing strength and courage from a Source that he knew he did not have. Sam listened in amazement as Grace pounded out an upbeat tune and then began to sing "Blessed Assurance," confidence and joy clear in her voice. It was at that moment that the words he'd been hearing every night for the past six weeks began repeating once more in his head, only this time it was just one simple phrase.

"For the wages of sin is death. For the wages of sin is death. For the wages of sin is death. For the . . . "

* * *

Grace finished the song with a flourish—her soul once more at peace—and she grabbed her Bible, stood up, and walked down from the platform. Intending to go get her purse and leave the church, she looked up toward her pew and froze when she saw the familiar man seated on the pew behind hers. She saw that his hands were clenching the back of her pew, his knuckles white, fingernails gripping the wood; and when she looked at his face, she saw in his warm, brown eyes the war that was being waged within him. Smiling gently, she walked to her pew and sat down, facing him. She kept silent, somehow knowing that it was the right thing to do, and prayed that evil would not win.

"You know that woman who got saved? The one you were praying with?" Sam asked after a very long silence.

"Yes," Grace answered quietly.

"She's the mother of the boy that had the roach stuck in his throat, the one I saved last week. She came to thank me for saving her son. I didn't want to be late again, so I just invited her to come with me. I was surprised when she agreed."

"I'm glad she did. Now her son will grow up to have a Christian mother, something that's important for every child."

"Do you remember when you asked me why I haven't been sleeping?"

"Vividly," Grace responded, for she had been concerned about him since learning he was not getting sleep.

"It was because of you."

"Of me?"

"During the day, I could ignore it. But at night when I didn't have anything else on my mind, I kept picturing your face in my mind and you'd look at me with such sad eyes, and you'd begin to speak to me."

"What did I say?"

"'For the wages of sin is death.' And you'd say it over and over again, all night long. It drove me insane. Then I'd talk to you in reality, and you started saying other things. Then finally, you said, *'For the wages of sin is death.* If you died today, do you know where you would spend eternity? You wouldn't go to Heaven; you'd go to Hell. Because you aren't saved. *But God commendeth his love toward us, in that, while we were yet sinners, Christ died for us.'* And you would repeat it, and I thought I was going crazy. During the day, if I did something wrong, I'd hear you recite whichever commandment I'd broken. When you sang that song about Jesus dying, I remembered our conversation about how He hadn't wanted to die but that He'd done it anyway; and as I watched you sing, I finally realized how you'd stayed so calm while talking to me about how little time you have left. And then when your father began to describe Hell . . . " Sam shivered and could not finish the sentence.

Grace was not surprised to find out that he'd been under conviction from the Holy Spirit for so long, but she wished he'd spoken to her long before now. Better late than never, she thought to herself and then took a deep breath. "So you brought the woman to church and she became convicted of her need for salvation, just as you've been convicted all of these six weeks; and she came forward and got saved. But, Sam, why didn't you come forward?"

"I couldn't seem to get out of my seat, and I kept thinking that this horrible tugging feeling and the overwhelming fear I had would eventually go away. And there were so many people around."

Grace put her hands on top of his and saw his eyes focus on her face. "There isn't anyone else here except for us. I can show you how to make the fear go away and that voice in your head stop."

"How could you do that?"

Grace smiled and said, "By leading you down the Roman's Road, Sam." Her smile widened when she watched tears slide down his cheeks. *Please, Lord, he's so close. Don't let him back out now.*

"Grace?"

"Yes, Sam?"

"I don't want to die and go to Hell and be separated from you forever. I want to go to Heaven, to be with you always. Please, show me what to do."

"Romans 3:10 says, 'As it is written, There is none righteous, no, not one.' Romans 3:23 says, 'For all have sinned, and come short of the glory of God.' Sam, do you believe that you're a sinner?"

"I *know* I am. Every time I broke a commandment, your voice was there to remind me of it."

"Romans 5:12 says, 'Wherefore, as by one man sin entered into the world, and death by sin; and so death passed upon all men, for that all have sinned.' Because we sin, there is a cost for that sin. And Romans 6:23 tells us what that cost is. 'For the wages of sin is death.' But the good news is that God has made a way for us to never have to pay that cost. He sent His Son, Jesus, to die on the cross as a perfect sacrifice. 'For the wages of sin is death; but the gift of God is eternal life through Jesus Christ our Lord.' So even though the wages of sin *is* death, through Jesus, we can have eternal life. And the reason why God did this is because He loves us more than we can possibly imagine. Romans 5:8 says, 'But God commendeth his love toward us, in that, while we were yet sinners, Christ died for us.' And in Romans 10:13, it says how easy it is for you to receive the gift of eternal life. 'For whosoever shall call upon the name of the Lord shall be saved.' Then in Romans 10:9, it says, 'That if thou shalt confess with thy mouth the Lord Jesus, and shalt believe in thine heart that God hath raised him from the dead, thou shalt be saved.' Sam, do you believe that Jesus is God's Son?"

"Yes, I do," Sam answered.

"Do you believe that Jesus lived a sinless life and died on the cross to save you from your sins?"

"I do," Sam replied.

"Do you believe that God raised Jesus from the dead?"

"Yes."

"Then all you need to do is pray and ask God to forgive you for your sins and ask Jesus to come into your heart to save you."

Sam bowed his head, closed his eyes, and began to pray. "God, I know I'm a sinner, and I'm sorry for the wrong I've done in my life. I believe You sent Your Son Jesus to die on the cross to save me from my sins and that He rose again. Please, forgive me and come into my heart to save me. I don't want to go to Hell, God. In Jesus' name I pray, amen." When Sam lifted his head back up to look at Grace, an amazing thing happened. He felt the choking fear, the tugging sensation, the worry, the repetitive verses, and the pain all melt away from him and be replaced by the most peaceful feeling he'd ever had. When he looked into Grace's eyes, it was as though he was seeing her for the very first time.

"Now, there's a passage I like to quote to new Christians so they will know that they can never lose their salvation. I know you've heard it before, but now you'll be able to understand it better. The passage is John 10:27-30, and in the passage, Jesus is speaking. He says, 'My sheep hear my voice, and I know them, and they follow me. And I give unto them eternal life; and they shall never perish, neither shall any man pluck them out of my hand. My Father, which gave them me, is greater than all and no man is able to pluck them out of my Father's hand. I and my Father are one.' No matter what you do now, you will always be a child of God and He will never forsake you."

"Grace?"

"Yes, Sam?"

"You were right not to agree to date me before. I did have a darkness in me."

"And now?"

"Now . . . now I feel . . . lighter, like I can breathe. And I don't feel afraid like I did before. It's difficult to describe."

"That is the feeling of true freedom, Sam. You're free of your guilt, your sin, your fears, your doubts, and your worries. It feels good, doesn't it?"

"It feels *wonderful*. I don't know why I didn't do this sooner. Grace, how would I go about getting baptized now?"

Grace beamed in response to his question. "If you come to tonight's service, when Dad gives the invitation, you come down, and someone will meet you at the front. Tell the person that you got saved and want to be baptized, and then they'll show you what you need to do from there." Grace grabbed her purse, rummaged around until she found an ink pen, then looked back at him. "Hand me your Bible, Sam."

Sam picked up his Bible and handed it to her, wondering what she was going to do, then sat silently as she wrote something inside of it. When he took it back, he saw she had written something beneath the note she'd previously written. It said, "Dr. Sam M. Gray: Born May 11, 1968, Born Again May 14,1993."

"That way, you'll never forget," Grace said softly.

Sam placed one of his hands atop one of hers, and staring deeply into her eyes, he said tenderly, "I love you, Grace."

"I love you, too, Sam."

* * *

Later that night, Grace took her prayer list and scratched out Sam's name from the "Unsaved" list, writing it beneath the "Other" list, her heart so full of joy that she felt as though she might burst. Before she began to pray for the unsaved on her list, she bowed her head and said aloud, "Heavenly Father, thank You for allowing me to see Sam saved before I die and for allowing me to be the one to lead him to You. Thank You for all You have done and all You have given to me, Lord. May You give Sam wisdom in the days and weeks ahead and comfort him and bring him Your perfect peace. Thank You again, Lord." Then she began to pray for those on her prayer list who still needed salvation.

* * *

Sam finished writing and then studied the prayer list he'd just made. It was short, for it didn't have very many names on it, but he knew that would change as time went by. He prayed for those on the list and then thanked God for saving his soul. Then he took his Bible and began reading in Genesis. He read ten chapters before he felt his eyes sag, and he knew he'd better stop and try to get some sleep. Before he put the Bible up, however, he said a final prayer. "God, I love Grace. You know I do. I love her so much that it hurts. And I know that if she dies, she'll go to Heaven. But even though it might be selfish of me to think this way, I don't want her to die. I want to spend as much time with her as I can, but I don't know what to do. Please, God, help me. Tell me what I should do about this."

Sam was about to put his Bible on the nightstand where he kept it when a sudden thought came into his mind. As he had once before, he opened his Bible and read the first verse that he saw. "'But if they cannot contain, let them marry: for it is better to marry than to burn,'" he read aloud. For a second time, he closed the Book, then opened it again and read the first verse he saw. "'House and riches are the inheritance of fathers: and a prudent wife is from the Lord.'" *Is that really what you want me to do, Lord?* he wondered. For a third and final time, he closed the Book, opened it, and read the first verse that he came across. "'Whoso findeth a wife findeth a good thing, and obtaineth favour of the Lord.'" Closing the Bible, he placed it on the nightstand, thoughts turning over in his head as he climbed into the bed, lay down, covered up, and stared up at the ceiling. "All right, Lord," he said into the quiet of the bedroom, "I'll ask her tomorrow."

When he closed his eyes, he saw her face in his mind; but instead of the sad look she usually had, she was smiling, her eyes shining, her face positively glowing. This time, she said nothing, and Sam was asleep within minutes, her smiling face fixed in his mind and a peace in his heart.

CHAPTER EIGHT

"For the Lord God is a sun and shield: the Lord will give grace and glory: no good thing will he withhold from them that walk uprightly."

Psalm 45:2

GRACE WAS IN HER CLASSROOM Monday afternoon doing her regular cleaning when she heard a knock on her door. Without stopping what she was doing, she called out, "Come in!" as she moved from student desk to student desk, wiping down the tops to get them ready for the next day. She heard the door open, but she didn't look up, wanting to hurry and finish so she could go home and have a little rest before she had to start dinner. The voice she heard stopped her instantly.

"Grace?"

Grace looked up from her cleaning to see Sam walking toward her; and when she saw the look on his face, she straightened up to her full height, recognizing that serious, determined look in his eyes. The last time she'd seen it on his face was the day he'd asked her out. Feeling her heart fluttering, she took a few deep breaths to try to calm herself; for this time, she would be able to say yes to him, and she silently thanked the Lord for the ability to do so. "Good afternoon, Sam," she said casually, a smile on her face. "You look like you've gotten some sleep."

"I did. No more 'For the wages of sin is death' going around and around in my head."

"I'm glad to hear it; I've been praying for you to get some good sleep. So from the look on your face, I'd say you're here for a specific reason instead of just a regular visit."

"Grace, I need to ask you something," Sam said.

A smile lifted the corners of her lips, and she watched him walk over to her. Her smile widened slightly when he reached out and took both of her hands in his.

"The day you gave me my Bible, before I went to bed that night, I argued with God. I was angry at Him for killing you after you'd been so obedient to Him, and I didn't understand how you could still love Him even after He allowed this to happen. So I did something that, at the time, I thought was silly, but maybe wasn't so silly after all. I opened up my Bible and read the first verse I saw. It only made me angrier because it was the 'For the wages of sin is death' verse that had been rattling around inside my head for so long. When I did it again, the verse was, 'But God commendeth his love for us, in that, while we were yet sinners, Christ died for us.' I did it a third time, and the verse I saw was, 'For whosoever shall call upon the name of the Lord shall be saved.' I had wanted answers, not realizing that to get them, I first had to be saved. It made me so angry, Grace. You can't imagine how angry I was."

"I understand. The lost don't have God inside them to help explain the Scriptures, so things often get muddled. It's easy to be angry and frustrated when you need answers but don't know how to find them. Now that you're saved, it will make it easier to understand the Bible, although some things, you might have to ask someone else about. But that's what your fellow Christians are for," she said gently, smiling at him.

"Last night, after I prayed for those on my prayer list and read some in my Bible, I prayed about you. I told God that I didn't want you to die, even though I know you'd go to Heaven, and I didn't know what to do, how to cope with losing you. I know I'm not supposed to think that way; I know I should want you to be in Heaven instead of here where you'd have to still deal with sin and danger, but I . . . I . . . "

Grace squeezed his hands then and said, "I know, Sam; I'm feeling the same way. I am excited that I'll see Heaven soon, that I'll finally meet my Savior face to face; but at the same time, I'm sad that I'll have to leave you and Dad and Esther and everyone else I've come to care for. There's nothing wrong with feeling that way." She knew it had been the right thing to say when she saw his shoulders relax a little, and she thanked God for giving her the right words to help him.

"After I prayed, I opened my Bible and read the first verse I saw. Then I did it a second and a third time. And I got the same answer every time. That's when I realized that before, I *had* been answered. God was trying to tell me that I needed to be saved before He could help. I felt this feeling of calm that I'd never had before, Grace, like I just knew that this was what God wants me to do. Do you want to know the verses I read? I don't remember what they say, but I wrote down the book, chapter, and verse so that I could tell you what they are. I figured you could quote them word for word."

"Go ahead, Sam," she said. She watched him take out a piece of notepaper and frowned when she saw his hands shaking. *Why would he be nervous about asking me out? He's already done it once; it isn't as though he thinks I'll say no now.*

"The first one I saw was 1 Corinthians 7:9," he said and waited to see if she'd recognize it.

"I know that one," she said instantly. "Dad preached a sermon once on that for the preacher boys we have in the church, all of whom are teenage boys. 'But if they cannot contain, let them marry: for it is better to marry than to burn.' It's about keeping you from fornicating."

"Fornicating?"

"Having sex outside of marriage. It's a sin." Grace saw Sam's face suddenly grow deep red, and she didn't know if it was from shame or embarrassment or both, but she wisely made no comment about it. "Basically, this verse is saying that if you're struggling to keep from fornicating with someone, it's better that you marry so you won't commit fornication, for it isn't a sin to have relations with your spouse."

"Okay, the burn part makes sense now," Sam said and felt his blush deepen. "The second verse I found was Proverbs 19:14."

Grace frowned, searching her memory, but came up with nothing. "Hmm, I can't recall that one. Let me look it up." She went to her teacher's desk, Sam following her, and she opened her Bible, flipping straight to Proverbs, for she kept a bookmark there since it was one of her favorite books of the Bible. "Proverbs 19 . . . ah, here it is. What verse was that?"

"Verse fourteen," he answered.

"Okay, here we go. Proverbs 19:14, 'House and riches are the inheritance of fathers: and a prudent wife is from the Lord.' I like this verse. I suppose I don't have to explain this one, since it's evident. What's the third verse?"

"This is my favorite, that much I do remember. It's Proverbs 18:22."

"That's another one I know. 'Whoso findeth a'—" She blinked then and straightened up to turn around and look at him, and when she looked into his warm brown eyes, she saw them dancing with joy and amusement. She felt heat surge through her when he lifted his hand and touched her face.

"'Whoso findeth a wife findeth a good thing, and obtaineth favour of the Lord,'" he quoted softly. "Grace, will you marry me?"

Grace was so stunned that she couldn't answer. She'd been prepared to be asked out on a date, but *this* was more than she'd ever dreamed of. *Please, God, help me find my voice!* she prayed. As if someone else was speaking out of her mouth, she gave him her answer. "'My beloved is mine, and I am his.'" Before she had time to react, he kissed her—a sweet, tender kiss on the lips—and for once in her life, Grace had no idea what to do, for it had been the first time she'd ever been kissed.

Sam held back, guided by a still, small Voice to be careful with her, to not overwhelm her, and so he gently ended the kiss much sooner than he wanted to. Staring into her eyes, he caressed her face, unable to speak for the emotions washing over him, and a fierce wave of love surged through him suddenly, so strong that it nearly brought him to his knees.

"I think—" Grace began, and her voice came out hoarse, and she had to clear her throat before trying again. "I think it would be best if . . . if . . . " She couldn't keep the thought long enough, her lips still tingling warmly from his kiss, and it became more difficult when she saw him smile lovingly at her.

"I understand, Grace," he said quietly. "I'm sorry I don't have an engagement ring for you right now, but I'll get one just as soon as I can, I promise." He saw her laugh just as tears began to drip from her eyes, and then she was shaking her head.

"I don't need an engagement ring, Sam," she told him. "A wedding band will be enough."

"Grace, how soon do you want to—"

"As soon as possible," she said instantly, knowing what he was about to ask. "Before your powers that be decide to reassign you. Besides, I want to spend what time I have left with you."

"I was hoping that would be your answer. I was thinking the same thing. The sooner you finish up here, the sooner we can go see your dad."

A huge smile spread over her face; and she went to the supply cabinet, grabbed the disinfectant and a second roll of paper towels, then came back to him. "I'll finish the desks; you get the blackboard."

He returned her smile, took the cleaning supplies, and said, "Yes, ma'am." He went to the blackboard as she went back to the desk she'd been working on when he'd arrived; but before he sprayed the board, he looked over at her. "And, Grace?"

"Yes, Sam?"

"You're getting an engagement ring," he said firmly, "even if you get the wedding band first."

* * *

Dr. Tanya Jackson walked into the makeshift break room and saw a sight she thought she'd never see.

Sitting at the folding table nearest the vending machines, Sam had his left hand around a can of soda, his right hand propping up his head, his eyes on the book opened in front of him.

Tanya knew that Sam wasn't much of a reader, so to find him reading on his lunch break was abnormal, to say the least. She said nothing at first, walking to the sandwich machine. After selecting the sandwich she wanted, she got herself a soda and then sat down opposite

Sam. She frowned when he didn't even look up; so she took the time to study his face, noting that the dark circles under his eyes were gone, the bags nearly so, as well as the worry lines that had creased his face for six weeks were gone. Looking into his eyes, she could clearly see a strange hunger but also a happiness that she'd not seen in him for a long time. She wondered what had happened to cause it, wondering if Grace had neglected to tell him her bad news. "Good book?" she finally asked him as she unsealed the container that held her sandwich.

Sam lifted his eyes and finally saw that he wasn't alone. "Tanya, I'm sorry. I didn't see you come in."

"So I noticed," she said, lips twitching in amusement. "So is it a good book?"

"None better," Sam answered happily.

"You seem to be feeling better. You're certainly looking a lot more rested. Are you finally getting sleep?"

"Yes, and this time, I'm actually sleeping the whole night through. I still have to catch up on all the sleep I've lost, but I will in time. And I'm feeling a lot better—better than I've ever felt."

"Well, I'm glad you're doing better. Everyone's been worried about you. I'm glad she didn't permanently break your heart."

The words confused Sam. "What do you mean?"

"You know what I mean. Little Miss—" Tanya caught herself, remembering what had happened the last time she'd called Grace that. "The Cloverdale woman."

Sam leaned back in his chair and stared at Tanya, knowing full well what she'd been about to call Grace. "Her name is Grace," Sam said clearly. "And you should know that, since you're monitoring her cancer's progression."

Wait; he knows? But how can he be so happy if he knows she's dying? I know he's angry with her, but he still wouldn't want her to die! This makes absolutely no sense! "She told you?" Tanya asked and couldn't keep the surprise from her voice.

"Of course, she told me. Why wouldn't she tell me?"

"Because you and she are fighting. And she specifically asked me not to say anything to you. Even made me promise, as though I'd break doctor-patient privacy laws. Infuriating woman, she is," Tanya said, muttering the last words to herself.

"Wow, office gossip is severely lagging," Sam said and found himself laughing, amused at the whole conversation.

"What are you talking about, Sam?"

"Grace and I aren't fighting," he said through his laughter. "Not even close! And she didn't want you to say anything to me because she didn't want me to worry about her."

"But you and she were fighting at the time."

"So? You think I'd stop worrying about her even though I was angry with her?"

"No . . . I suppose you wouldn't. But, Sam, she broke your heart, I know she did. I saw it on your face all last week. You shouldn't have anything more to do with her. She'll hurt you again."

Sam couldn't help it; he began to laugh harder, and then he was shaking his head, trying to stop the laughter. "No, she didn't," he said, managing to bring the laughter down to a chuckle. "It was the other way around. But it doesn't matter now."

"Now wait a minute, Sam. I *saw* you walking around here like a zombie! You wouldn't talk to anyone, wouldn't smile, wouldn't eat. If you hurt her, you wouldn't have acted like the walking wounded."

Sam realized that Tanya was worried for him, and so he sighed, knowing she wouldn't let it go. "Do you remember the warning you gave me before? About how she wouldn't want anything to do with me and that if I pursued a relationship, she'd break my heart?"

"Yeah," Tanya said.

"Well, I asked her out, and she said no."

"I tried to tell you."

"But she didn't say no because she wanted to. She said no because of her beliefs. And she never led me on or intended to hurt me. When she tried to explain, I was too stubborn, and I refused to listen. All of those weeks of seeing how sweet and gentle she was, of how caring and kind and considerate, and I just ignored that and stormed out of there like an idiot. I spent all last week miserable and angry and confused; and I was so stubborn, I refused to go back. I didn't want to see her again, didn't want to hear her voice. Well, when instead of me, Dr. Williamson arrived in my place and explained to her that I wouldn't be coming back, Grace decided to come to me instead of waiting for me to stop being stupid. She told me she loved me—"

"She's got a funny way of showing it," Tanya said in disapproval and saw Sam frown at her.

"—and finally, when I let her, she explained why she'd said no when I'd asked her out. Once I realized that she hadn't been trying to hurt me and that she hadn't wanted to tell me no, I realized how dumb I'd been to think she'd ever wanted to hurt me."

"Sam—"

"No, let me finish. Her faith kept her from saying yes, and I respected her beliefs, even though I didn't understand them. And because of that, she and I reconciled."

"So you started dating then?"

"No, because she couldn't go against her beliefs."

"Let me guess," Tanya said, her voice harsh. "Something about being unequally yoked together with unbelievers. Am I right?"

Sam was surprised and said, "Yes. How did you know that?"

"My parents dragged me to church every Sunday and Wednesday. It was drilled into my head."

"I wish my parents had. Though honestly, I don't know that I would've listened then."

Tanya frowned and took a bite of her sandwich, deciding to ignore what he'd just said. "Okay, so you and she aren't dating, but you aren't fighting either. So, what are you so . . . *Oh*, I see. Well, no wonder you look so relaxed," Tanya said and then started snickering.

It wasn't the words she'd said but the way she'd said them that made Sam pick up on the innuendo. He sat there and stared at her silently for a moment, trying to control the anger he was feeling, and prayed for help. "I'm going to pretend that I don't understand what you're implying, but let me be very clear. I understand that you don't like her—and I think I know why—but that does not give you the right to talk about her the way you are. She hasn't insulted you, yelled at you, gossiped about you, or hurt you in any other way; and the way you're acting is extremely petty and childish. And even though it's none of your business, I am not about to let anyone think she's a hypocrite or believe that she's anything less than honorable, so *no*, Tanya, you don't see why I am so relaxed."

"Sam, I—"

"For the past six weeks, I've gone home and tried to go to sleep, but all I kept hearing were Bible verses running through my mind.

The words wouldn't leave me alone, and I felt like I was going insane The more time went by, the worse it became. Even after Grace and I resolved our misunderstanding, it kept getting worse and worse; and I wanted to talk to her about it, but something always kept me from it. Then when I found out Grace had cancer and was dying, I got angry. Not a little but a lot. I was angry that she'd obeyed God only to have Him do this to her. I couldn't understand why He would punish her after she'd done everything He'd asked of her. She tried to explain to me that it wasn't a punishment but a reward, but I didn't believe that for a second. And then I watched as she went through the weekend, and even though she was afraid, she remained strong and continued to serve her God and love Him. I'd never seen anyone take that kind of news and find happiness in it, but she did. It was the most amazing thing I'd ever seen, Tanya. It was like she had infinite reserves of peace and comfort, and I couldn't figure out how she could be so calm about it all. Until Sunday morning when I went to church and I watched her get up in front of the church and sing. I *watched* as she gathered that inner strength of hers, saw the peace come over her face to get her through the song without breaking down into tears. It finally dawned on me where it came from. It didn't come from her— although at first, that's what I'd thought. It came from her faith, from her belief that God was in complete control and knew what was best for her."

"Sam, listen to me—"

"Tanya, she stood up in front of the church and announced to them that she had inoperable breast cancer and had been given only eight months to live. And do you know what she did?"

"I can't even guess."

"She's the one who will have to suffer, the one who will die, and yet *she* comforted *them*. She asked them for only three things. She asked them to pray for her and her family, to pray for her students, and she . . . " Sam's voice broke then as he remembered how she'd looked, what she'd said. "She asked them to pray for me to be saved, telling them I would need God's comfort after she was gone. She wasn't concerned about herself, Tanya; she was concerned about everyone she'd be leaving behind. She told me that afternoon that the day she found out she had cancer and that nothing could be done about it, she'd asked God for only one thing before she died. And you know, He gave it to her."

"Uh huh, and what exactly did she ask for?"

Sam took his Bible and turned it to the page where Grace had written his date of birth and the date of his salvation, and he turned the Book around and pointed at the words. "She asked God to allow her to see me accept Jesus into my heart," he said. "That was on Friday. She had to wait only two days."

"Wait, what?" Tanya asked, startled now, and she saw that the Book he'd been reading was the Bible; and she read what Grace had written in his Bible, stopping on the words "born again." Having grown up in church, Tanya knew what that meant.

"But He not only allowed her to see me saved; He also allowed her to be the one to lead me to Him."

"Please tell me you did it just to be with her. Please, Sam, tell me you were just humoring her." But Tanya could see it on his face even before he spoke.

"You know me better than that. If I was going to do that, I would've done it long before now. I told her that I wouldn't get saved just to be with her, that it would be dishonest, and I wasn't going to do that. She didn't want me to either. No, Tanya, I didn't do it for her. I did it for *me*. And the moment I did, I felt all of the anger and worry and pain lifted off of me. That night was the first night I'd slept in weeks. And now when I look at her, it's like I never really saw her and appreciated her before, and I love her so much more now than I did before."

"She has brainwashed you," Tanya said then, feeling anger come over her.

Sam laughed. "No, she didn't. God did; and let me tell you, my brain definitely needed a good washing, right along with my heart."

"That's not what I meant," she snapped.

"I know what you meant. Next time you see her, watch her and how she handles situations, how she deals with her impending death. It's *real*, Tanya, and so is God."

"That's just what you want to think. You're trying to cope with the fact that she's dying, and so you're grasping at whatever you can to help you through it. And when she dies—"

"She's not going to die."

"Now, don't start on that eternal life nonsense!"

"No, I don't mean that, although it isn't nonsense. I mean the cancer isn't going to kill her."

"Did she even show you the mammogram? The—"

"Oh, she still thinks she is going to die from the cancer. But I know she isn't."

"And what makes you say that?"

"Because I'm praying she'll be cured of it. While I know that's no guarantee, I just have this . . . feeling that she's going to be all right."

"Sam, you are delusional and irrational. You need to take some time off and recover from all the sleep you've lost and the shock of her diagnosis because you obviously aren't dealing well with it at all."

"Come to church Sunday," Sam said.

"Sam, God is a myth," Tanya said firmly.

"You're an atheist?" he asked in surprise, having never discussed faith with her.

"Yes, I am and proud of it, too." She frowned when he took a pen out of the pocket of his doctor's coat, turned his Bible to where he had a piece of paper, and began to write something down on the paper. "What are you doing?"

"Writing your name down."

"For what?"

"So that I can pray for you."

Tanya scowled and said, "I don't want you to pray for me."

"I'm going to anyway, though." He put his list back into his Bible and the ink pen back in his coat pocket.

Tanya was about to say something when she heard a voice from behind her.

"Sam! Sam, I've got them!"

Tanya turned around and watched as Grace Cloverdale came rushing into the room, her arms filled with small squares of pale yellow paper with gold edging. Frowning at Grace's presence, knowing the woman should not be back here, she opened her mouth to say something about it. But before she could, she saw Sam get up and move his Bible over to the place beside his.

"Wow, Esther got them done faster than I thought she would," Sam remarked. "Here, sit down, and we'll split up the ones that go to my coworkers."

"I already gave Laura hers. She promised to be there. She's so excited!" Grace said as she sat down. "And Esther worked on them most of the night."

"Wait, aren't you supposed to be teaching class right now?" Sam asked then and saw her smile.

"Esther is taking them for the rest of the week, since I'm going to be busy."

"I wish *I* could take off for the rest of the week," Sam lamented.

Grace smiled ruefully and said, "I wish you could, too. I could definitely use more help. But I've called some of the ladies in the church, and they're helping me so everything will get done soon enough."

"I hate to break up this conversation," Tanya said insincerely, "but Miss Cloverdale, you aren't supposed to be back here."

"Laura said it was all right, that Sam was on lunch and that I wouldn't be interfering with his work." Grace looked at Sam and asked, "You won't get in trouble, will you? I don't want to get you in trouble with—"

"Don't worry about it, Grace; I won't get in trouble."

"Okay, good. And, Dr. Grayson, I'm glad you're here. Let's see . . . I know it's here somewhere . . . Ah, here it is. This is yours," Grace said and handed the paper out to the female doctor. "We would be having it on a Saturday, but Sam has to work, so it'll be at one o'clock this Sunday. I hope you can come."

Tanya took the piece of paper and read it, her eyes growing wide as she realized she was holding a handmade wedding invitation.

When she looked back up from it, she stared directly at Sam. "Why so soon, Sam?"

"We want to be married before I get reassigned."

"That could be months from now," Tanya said.

"Or it could be tomorrow or next week," he remarked.

"Wouldn't help if it was tomorrow, though." Tanya saw him smile and got the odd feeling that he'd anticipated her words.

"That's why her father agreed to marry us at a moment's notice. All we have to do is call him and let him know."

"Then why wait until Sunday?" Tanya asked.

"I want her to have a nice wedding. I don't like that it has to be rushed, and I don't like that she can't invite half of the people she wants to because they're all back in the States. I also don't like that she can't go shopping for wedding dresses to pick the one she wants, but there's nothing I can do about any of that. So I'm doing all I can to give her as close to a picture-perfect wedding as I possibly can."

"I don't need a picture-perfect wedding, Sam," Grace said softly, smiling lovingly at him. "And as for a dress, that's been taken care of."

"Already? That was fast!" Sam said.

"Just wait until you see it."

"Sam, this is a mistake," Tanya said.

Grace tilted her head and silently studied the black-haired woman, able to feel the seething rage coming from her.

"It was a mistake getting mixed up with her from the very start, and now, it's gone too far. I told you what would happen, and it did. And now you want to marry her just to get under her skirt when there are plenty of—"

Sam stood to his feet, his eyes darkening with anger and indignation, his whole body shaking with the rage that was coursing through him. "How dare you say that," he said through clenched teeth.

"Oh, come on, it's not so farfetched. It's actually quite perfect. Marry her now to get what you want, since she's a prude—and it's the only way she'll agree—and when she dies, find someone else who isn't so demanding. You won't even have to put up with her for very long since—"

"You'd better be thanking God that you're not a man right now," Sam said, "because if you were, I'd—"

"Sam," Grace said calmly and stood up to put a hand on his shoulder.

Sam looked at her then; and when he saw those still-calm eyes, it helped to calm him down, too. "It isn't like that, Grace."

"I know, Sam."

"She has no right to say things like that, to trivialize and cheapen my love for you."

"'Blessed are ye, when men shall revile you, and persecute you, and shall say all manner of evil against you falsely, for my sake. Rejoice, and be exceeding glad: for great is your reward in heaven: for so persecuted they the prophets which were before you,'" Grace said softly to him. "Remember, not so long ago, you were in her place." When she felt him relax beside her, she turned her eyes toward Tanya. "In your attempt to hurt me, you have just accused your own friend of having dishonorable intentions toward me, of having a dishonest reason for marrying me, and for taking perverse advantage of the fact that I don't have long to live. A true friend would never have done that."

The gentle admonishing called attention to Tanya's failure to offend Grace, and the black-haired woman was not happy at all to be on the receiving end of Grace's calm reproof, for there was really no way she could justify what she'd just said to Sam. Grace's next words just made it even worse.

"Because I know where your words come from, I forgive you for saying them, and I will be praying for you." Grace turned back to Sam. "Sam, if you still want her at the wedding, she is welcome to come if she wishes."

"You'd still be willing to have her there even after what she said?"

"Ephesians 4:32 says, 'And be ye kind one to another, tenderhearted, forgiving one another, even as God for Christ's sake hath forgiven you,'" Grace told him.

"You're amazing, Grace," he said to her and felt warmth flood through him when she smiled.

"I've got to deliver the rest of the invitations, so I need to go, but I'll see you later tonight at the house. Oh, and just so you know, Esther wants a rematch on *Sorry!* from the other night so be prepared."

Sam chuckled and gathered up the invitations for his coworkers. "Tell her I said bring it on."

Grace laughed and then pointed at one of the invitations in his hands. "Do you like them, by the way?"

Sam looked at one, read it, then looked back at her and smiled. "Esther did a good job. Before you tell her that I said bring it on, tell her thank you for me."

"I will. I love you."

"I love you, too. See ya tonight." Sam waited until she was gone before he turned his focus back upon Tanya. "You can say what you want to about me; I don't care, but if you ever speak that way about her again, you will lose a friend."

"Aren't you supposed to be forgiving?" Tanya sneered.

"I can forgive you without keeping you as a friend. Remember that the next time you think of speaking against her." Then Sam picked up his Bible, and with his arms full, he left the makeshift breakroom, praying for Tanya's salvation and praying that God would help him conquer the anger he felt for the unsaved woman.

"Nervous?"

The question came from behind Sam, causing him to turn around to see Thomas Cloverdale dressed in a white dress shirt and a light gray suit jacket, slacks, and matching tie walking into the room where Sam was waiting. "That word doesn't even begin to describe what I'm feeling right now," he admitted. "I never knew anyone could feel scared to death and completely at peace all at the same time, but that's exactly how I feel."

Thomas clapped the younger man supportively on the shoulder, chuckling softly at the young doctor's admission. "Ah, yes, I remember that feeling," the pastor said, nodding. "It got so bad, I thought I would pass out. It only got worse when I went to stand up at the front by the pastor and wait for the procession, and the wait felt like forever."

"Worse? You're telling me it'll get worse? I don't think I can take much more!" Sam exclaimed.

"Don't worry, Son. As soon as you see her walking down that aisle, you'll forget the fear, and all you'll be able to think about is how blessed you are to be marrying the sweetest, most beautiful woman to ever live. At least, that's what happened to me when I got married."

"I wish we could've done this right," Sam said, sighing. "I wish we'd had more time to plan this. There are so many people I know Grace wanted here, and I would've loved to have my parents here. I mean, I haven't even gotten her an engagement ring. I feel like I'm doing this all wrong."

"Sam," Thomas said calmly, "you said that you know this is the right decision, yes?"

"Well, yes, but—"

"Grace feels the same way. She wishes there was more time and that your parents could be here, too, but she has prayed since you asked her to marry you and is certain that this—that *you*—are what God had planned for her life. God does not make mistakes, and since you know you are doing what God wants you to, that means you aren't doing this all wrong."

Sam nodded silently, feeling the worry loosen its grip on him just a little. "Thank you, Dr. Cloverdale," he said. "I'm just so nervous."

"Don't worry; I'm sure Grace is just as nervous."

Sam chuckled and replied, "I doubt that. I can't imagine her being nervous about anything. She's always so calm about everything."

"Oh, she has her moments, believe me. Anyway, I came to tell you that it's time to take your place. I'm about to go tell her, too."

"I wish she was standing here right now. She'd be able to calm me down for sure."

"Go on now, Son, and don't worry. It'll be over before you know it."

"Okay, but she'd better hurry, or she might find me passed out at the altar!" Sam replied as he watched the pastor leave the room. Just before he stepped out of the Sunday school room, Sam took a deep breath in and slowly breathed it back out again. Bowing his head and closing his eyes, he began to pray. "God, please help me not to make a mistake today; help me to calm down; and help me not to pass out at the altar. Most of all, though, please help me to be a good, godly husband to her. In Jesus' name I pray, amen." Then taking one more deep breath in, he walked out of the room, down the aisle of the crowded auditorium, and to the altar to stand and wait, hands shaking and heart pounding.

* * *

Thomas knocked softly on one of the Sunday school doors and smiled when he heard Esther immediately ask who it was. "Your dad," he said through the door and didn't need to wait long before she opened it and peeked out.

"Are you alone?" Esther eyed him suspiciously, her hazel eyes glancing around.

Thomas laughed. "Of course I am. Are you two ready yet? I hope you are because I just sent the groom up to the altar to wait."

"We're ready, Dad," Esther said and opened the door to let him in.

Thomas walked in and grinned when he heard Esther immediately close the door behind him. He looked toward the woman in white and gasped softly as she turned to face him.

"Well?" Grace asked and smiled gently as tears filled her father's eyes.

"You look just like your mother did when I married her," Thomas' voice came out hoarse. "Are you nervous?"

Grace laughed softly at the question. "I've never been more nervous in my entire life than I am right now."

"Not that she's showing it, though." Esther smiled.

"Well, your groom is at the altar waiting and I've come to tell you it's time. Are you ready, Grace?"

Grace smiled. "I've never been more ready for something than I am right now, Dad."

Thomas chuckled at her answer and moved so he could look at both of his daughters. "I'm proud of you—both of you—and I know I say it all the time, but I am thankful God gave me such wonderful, beautiful daughters. I love you both very much."

"I love you, too, Dad!" Esther said exuberantly.

"And I love you, too, Dad," Grace said in her characteristically calm voice.

"Go wait out in the hall for your sister, Esther," Thomas requested.

"Ooo, I'm so excited! It's almost time!" Esther practically squealed and then left the room.

Thomas studied Grace's appearance silently for a few more moments and then took her hands in his. There were so many things he wanted to say but couldn't find the words to express them to her. He saw her smile and felt her squeeze his hands, then move to put her arms around him.

"It's all right, Dad," she said. "I already know."

"I love you, Grace."

"I love you, too, Daddy. Thank you for everything you've done for me, everything you taught me."

He hugged her tightly to him and then forced himself to let her go. "Come on; you've got an anxious groom waiting for you. If you don't get out there soon, he might pass out."

Grace laughed and blinked back tears, then nodded at him. "I'll be out there soon."

"All right then. Give me a little bit to get up there. You really do look beautiful."

"Thank you, Daddy." Grace waited until her father had left before she went to the door. Taking a bouquet of wildflowers from a nearby chair, she took a single deep breath in and let it out slowly. Raising her eyes, she prayed, "Lord, don't let me make any mistakes today, and help Sam get through the ceremony without passing out. More than anything else, please help me to be a good wife to Sam for as long as I live. In Jesus' name, amen." Then she walked out of the room to join her waiting twin sister and listened for the cue from the pianist.

* * *

When Sam saw Grace's father walking down the aisle to take his place, Sam's heart began to race with anticipation, knowing that this agonizing wait was nearly over. Sam heard the piano music change and watched as first one and then another African woman came walking up the aisle, and Sam recognized both ladies as members of the church, both of whom he knew had been led to the Lord by Grace. When both ladies took their places on the bride's side, Sam saw a third person step out and walk down the aisle, and this person he knew personally. He grinned at young Tinashe as she walked up the aisle holding a little basket from which she took flower petals and scattered them all along the aisle as she came. As soon as the little girl came to the end of the aisle, she grinned at Sam, giggling when he winked back at her, and then took her place near the bridesmaids. As soon as Sam heard the pianist play the introduction to "The Wedding March," Sam's eyes darted to the end of the aisle, and he held his breath, his heart pounding loudly in his ears. He saw Esther in one of Grace's pastel pink church dresses step out into the aisle, a huge grin upon her face; and then in the next instant, all he could see was the breathtaking woman in white.

"Breathe, Sam," Thomas advised in a low voice.

Sam realized he was still holding his breath, so he let it go and breathed back in again as he watched her take Esther's proffered arm and then walk up the aisle toward him, her eyes locked with his the entire time. *Please, God, make me worthy of her,* he prayed silently as she came. In that moment, he saw a brilliant smile come over her face; and he had the sudden urge to go to her, wrap his arms around her, and kiss her right then—she looked so beautiful—but he resisted the urge. Soon, she was standing beside him, those beautiful eyes of hers staring into his through the white veil she wore.

Esther took hold of Sam's left hand and gently placed Grace's right hand into it, giving Sam a sunny smile. "Take care of her, Sam."

"I will, I promise," he replied, his eyes never leaving Grace's.

Esther hugged Grace once and then moved to stand by the other bridesmaids.

* * *

Grace smiled up at Sam, her heart beating wildly out of control, and felt Sam reach his other hand out for hers until he held both of her hands in his.

"You look . . . so beautiful, Grace." Sam found it difficult to speak. His heart skipped a few beats when her smile widened, and he saw unshed tears glistening in her eyes.

"'His eyes are as the eyes of doves by the rivers of waters, washed with milk, and fitly set,'" she responded softly, and there was no disguising the love in her voice or her eyes.

"Ready?" he asked her.

"I've never been more ready for anything else in my life, Sam," she answered just as she had her father. "Are you?"

"Absolutely," he responded with surety in his voice. "Let's get married."

She laughed softly, and then they both turned to her father and nodded to indicate their readiness to begin.

Thomas smiled at them both and then began the ceremony. "Dearly beloved, we are gathered here today in the presence of God to join this man and this woman in holy matrimony . . . "

* * *

As soon as Sam opened his front door, his nostrils were assailed by a most welcoming aroma, and he couldn't help but smile. His smile didn't last long, however, and so it was with a heavy sigh that he closed and bolted the front door behind him. Absently, he dropped the truck keys on the nearest table before heading toward the small room that served as his kitchen, and a second smile lifted the corners of his mouth as he heard lighthearted humming just before he reached the kitchen doorway. His smile widened at the sight that met his eyes, and he leaned against the doorway in silence just to enjoy it before he had to spoil everything.

Grace stood with her back to the door, oblivious to the fact that she was being observed, her attention focused on the large stew pot on the stove in front of her and its bubbling contents. Reaching for several spices and seasonings, she added them one by one while she stirred the food with a spoon she held in her other hand. Once she was finished, she transferred the stirring spoon to her right hand and used it to bring a taste of the liquid up to her lips. Pausing in her humming, she tasted the concoction, and,nodding to herself in satisfaction, she put the lid back on to let it finish cooking. She set the stirring spoon aside and bent to peek into the oven, picking up her humming right where she'd left off.

My wife, Sam marveled to himself, as he did each time he was reminded that he was a happily married man now. *Thank You, Lord, for bringing me here and for throwing us together.* Sam's smile faded once more then as the burden on his heart came rushing back. *Please, God, don't let her cry. I don't think I could handle it if she cries,* he prayed silently.

"Ah!" exclaimed Grace then, for she'd turned to set the table for dinner, two bowls in one hand and two spoons in the other, when she saw Sam standing in the doorway watching her, startling her. "Sam, don't *do* that! You scared me to death!"

"I didn't mean to. It smells good, Grace," he told her and watched as her eyes lit up and her cheeks practically glowed with joy at his compliment.

"Thank you. It's almost ready to eat." Grace studied his face for a moment and then asked, "What's wrong?"

"It can wait until after dinner."

"Best to get it out of the way now. Besides, I don't want to watch you worry all the way through dinner," she reasoned.

"You aren't going to be happy," he warned her.

"Whatever it is will be worked out by God for our good and His glory, Sam; now tell me what's wrong."

"We got word today that we're to leave on Monday morning for Haiti," he revealed miserably.

After a few moments of silence to digest the news and gather her thoughts, she responded thoughtfully. "Hmm, I've never been to Haiti. I can't wait to see it."

"You . . . you're not upset?" Sam asked in disbelief, staring skeptically into her eyes for any signs she was hiding her true feelings.

"I'm surprised you've been reassigned so soon; I'm wondering if my dad will be able to find a replacement for me on such short notice, but I'm not upset," she answered honestly.

"You'll have to leave your home and church; you'll have no school to teach at, and who knows how long it'll be before you see your family again. Doesn't any of that bother you?"

"It wouldn't matter where I went; that would all happen to me sooner or later," she said calmly, alluding to the cancer he still didn't like to acknowledge.

Sam went to her and put his hands on her shoulders, staring down into those shocking blue-green eyes of hers. "Grace, I don't want to take you away from your family. This whole situation is a disaster, and I wish there was a way for me to fix this so we could stay here until . . . " Sam didn't finish the sentence, knowing he didn't need to.

"'And we know that all things work together for good to them that love God, to them who are the called according to his purpose,'" she quoted, knowing Romans 8:28 was now one of his favorite verses.

"I know, and I've prayed about this since I was told. I know this is what God wants, but I don't understand why He'd want me to take you from your family at a time when you need them most."

"'But he said, Yea rather, blessed are they that hear the word of God, and keep it,' Luke 11:28. Sam, God doesn't require us to understand why He wants us to do something. He requires only our obedience."

"I know. I just . . . didn't expect this to happen so soon. Grace, I really am sorry about this. I know how much your family means to you and—"

"'I am my beloved's, and my beloved is mine,'" she told him tenderly.

"I've heard that one, I think."

A sly grin stole across her face, and she answered, "Song of Solomon 6:3a."

Sam knew that was the end of the conversation when she began quoting from Song of Solomon, so he nodded. "Okay, I give up."

"God wouldn't send you somewhere He wouldn't want me to go. We are one flesh. We'll know the reason He's doing this when He wants us to know. Okay?"

Sam touched her cheek and smiled at her. "You're amazing, Grace, and I don't deserve you," he told her quietly before he kissed her.

* * *

"That's impossible. Have you checked your equipment?"

"Yes, three times," was the answer through the phone, spoken in the man's native Swahili language.

Tanya sat and stared at an x-ray film, confused and unhappy, an unsettling feeling in the pit of her stomach. "Maybe it was mixed up with someone else's—"

"It wasn't," the male voice on the phone interrupted in a firm tone. "I made certain of that. Believe me, I don't understand it any more than you do."

"But it's *impossible*," Tanya said again, mostly to herself as she tried to make sense out of the insensible. From far back in her past, a long-forgotten memory resurfaced, and she could hear her mother just as clearly now as she had on the day she'd heard the words.

"*'But Jesus beheld them, and said unto them, With men this is impossible; but with God all things are possible.'*"

Tanya blinked a few times as her brain tried to process the situation she was now in and then asked, "Today is Wednesday, isn't it?"

"For the remainder of the day, yes."

"Thank you for taking my call so late in the day," she said.

"You're welcome. Have a good evening."

"Thank you. You, too," she returned and hung up the phone. Tanya took the x-rays, gathered up their accompanying papers, and hurriedly but carefully stuffed them back into the large manila envelope they'd come to her in. Grabbing her purse from the floor nearby, she snuck a peek at the watch on her wrist and knew she'd have to hurry if she was going to reach her destination on time.

Tanya felt uncomfortable as she walked into the church lobby, and she had to force herself not to clench the medical papers she held in her hand. It had been years since she'd set foot inside a church, and she wasn't too pleased she was there; but she didn't want to wait any longer to do what she knew she had to do.

"Welcome to Lighthouse Baptist Church," a well-dressed man greeted her pleasantly in Swahili. "We are so glad you are here with us this evening."

"Umm, thanks," Tanya said in a tense voice. "Has the service begun yet? I need to speak with Grace Gray if I could."

"The service is just beginning, but I'm sure Sister Grace will be available afterward. Come, I'll show you to a seat."

"Oh, I don't want to disturb the service," Tanya said, feeling a desperate need to flee now.

"You won't," he assured her with a big smile as he opened the door to the auditorium. "Right this way please."

Before she knew what was happening, she found herself following him to an empty pew in the central section of the auditorium as the congregation sang the old hymn, "Onward, Christian Soldiers." She thanked the usher and picked up a hymnal, opened the burgundy book to a random song, and began to sing without looking at the pages. She remembered the song in its entirety and didn't need the hymnal, but she didn't want to feel any more out of place than she already did.

After a few more songs, the song leader bade everyone to take their seats, and once everyone had, he addressed the congregation with a pleasant smile. "We have a special for you tonight I believe you will enjoy."

Tanya saw him motion to someone on the left side of the auditorium, and she watched a couple on the front row stand up together and make their way up to the platform to stand at the pulpit. Her eyes widened when the couple faced the crowd and she recognized Sam and Grace. She had never seen Sam in a suit and tie before, and it was just more proof of how much the missionary's daughter had changed him.

"Just so you know," Grace stated clearly into the pulpit's microphone, "the song selection was Sam's choice, not mine."

Tanya saw Sam give his wife a devilish grin, and then as the introduction began to play, she heard the congregation laugh knowingly. Tanya didn't catch on to the joke until she heard Sam's rich baritone begin the first verse of "Amazing Grace." *I didn't even know he could sing,* she thought to herself as she listened to the words of the well-known hymn. A second shock ran through her when Grace sang the second verse, and Tanya noticed how bright and joyful the expression was on the missionary daughter's face. The physician searched for any sign of stress, worry, or fear that would betray Grace's thoughts and feelings beneath the façade; but she could find none. Tanya could not understand how someone with so much to live for and every reason to be afraid or angry at God could continue to praise Him with no hesitation.

"*It's real, Tanya, and so is He,*" Sam had told her right after he'd gotten saved, the memory strong in her mind.

As Sam and Grace blended their voices together for the rest of the song, Tanya began to wonder if everything she'd learned at her parents' church had actually been the truth, and it had been she who'd been deceived into believing a lie. The thought made her squirm in her seat and even more desperate to leave the church than before; but she stayed where she was, and when the singers were finished and had gone to their pew, Tanya forced herself to calm down.

Grace's father came up to the pulpit then, holding his Bible and smiling at his daughter and son-in-law. Setting the precious Book down and opening it to where his text was, he complimented the singers on their performance and welcomed everyone to the service. Then he said, "Before we pray and ask God for His blessing on the preaching tonight, we'll take some prayer requests."

Tanya listened to those who raised their hands in response, but it wasn't until after Dr. Cloverdale had called his daughter's name that Tanya paid any real attention. Tanya thought the missionary's daughter would remind her fellow churchgoers to continue to pray for her health and family, but that wasn't what Grace did.

"Sam has received word that he and his coworkers will be leaving for Haiti this coming Monday morning, so we're asking for traveling mercies for us," Grace stated, projecting her voice so that she could be heard in the large room.

Tanya saw Grace smile down at Sam before taking a deep breath and continuing.

"Sam and I also covet your prayers for the health of the baby God has seen fit to bless us with." Grace grinned as Sam took one of her hands in his in a loving gesture. "We aren't sure how this will work out—with my cancer—but we trust God knows what He is doing better than we ever could. Thank you, everyone, and may God bless you all."

Tanya stared at the manila envelope, and it was like the last piece of a puzzle had dropped into place. *I understand now,* she thought silently.

"Well," said Thomas into the microphone, "congratulations to you both." He looked out upon the sea of faces and called, "Any other prayer requests or blessings?" A single hand raised in the air, and as soon as the missionary saw it, he began to pray the person would be saved before the service dismissed that night. "Dr. Jackson, it's good to see you this evening. You have a prayer request?"

Grace and Sam turned to find the unexpected visitor slowly standing. They both began praying she would accept Jesus as her Savior this night, giving no other thought as to what had brought her to the service.

"Ordinarily, I wouldn't do this, but I know she won't mind." Tanya turned to where Grace and Sam sat together and saw them watching her. "Grace, your last test results came in late today, but I thought there had to be some type of mistake because these kinds of things just don't happen. The technician I spoke with confirmed that the results are accurate. The cancer . . . It's gone."

"Gone?" Grace repeated, stunned beyond belief, certain she'd misheard.

"Yes," Tanya said. "It's like it was never there at all, though I know for certain it was."

"So I'm not dying?" Grace asked, needing to hear the doctor say the words.

"No more than the rest of us are," Tanya answered.

As Grace and Sam hugged each other, tears streaming down their faces, and the rest of the congregation began to finally react to this most welcome news, Tanya sat back down, feeling completely drained of energy. She was relieved to have gotten done what she'd come to do.

"Well," Thomas said from the pulpit, just as shocked as everyone else, "I think we need another song before I start preaching." The song leader once more led them in a hymn, the upbeat "Blessed Assurance," and then the missionary came back to the pulpit to give the sermon.

When Thomas gave the altar call that night, the first one to step into the aisle was Tanya. When she reached the front, she was met by the sincere smile of the woman she had ridiculed, disrespected, and hated. "I want what you have," Tanya told the missionary's daughter. "I want to know Jesus."

As she had done with so many others before, Grace took her Bible and led her doctor down the Roman's Road to salvation.

* * *

Grace and Sam made it safely to Haiti, where Sam would continue his humanitarian aid and where Grace found a church her own home church in Missouri supported. They both attended faithfully, and it wasn't long before Grace began to teach, both in the church and the school. After several months of doing God's work there, they learned Grace would be having triplets, and after much prayer and discussion, made the decision to go back to Missouri for the safety of the mother and the babies.

On a cold, windy morning in the middle of January, instead of attending a funeral for his wife, Sam and Grace were instead rejoicing and thanking God for the safe delivery of their three newborn daughters.

"What are we going to name them, Sam?" Grace asked as she held two of the three babies in her arms as she rested in the hospital bed.

"I've been thinking about that," Sam said. "What about Faith, Hope, and Charity?"

Grace laughed softly and looked down at her babies. "Those are good names. You do know what those three attributes are sometimes called, don't you?"

"No."

"They are sometimes known as the three Christian graces."

"Well, then we *have* to give them those names," Sam stated firmly, grinning as he stared into his wife's eyes.

"I love you, Sam," she said softly to him.

"I love you, too," he responded in kind. Caressing her cheek, he added, "You're amazing, Grace," just before he bent to kiss her.

THE END

AUTHOR'S NOTE

HEAVEN OR HELL? IF YOU DIED TODAY, DO YOU KNOW
WHERE YOU WOULD SPEND ETERNITY?

In the course of reading this book, if you have realized you are not saved and you would like to be, please don't wait any longer! "Whereas ye know not what shall be on the morrow. For what is your life? It is even a vapour, that appeareth for a little time, and then vanisheth away" (James 4:14).

To receive Jesus into your heart, you must first admit to God that you have sinned. Romans 3:10 says, "As it is written, There is none righteous, no, not one." You must truly be sorry that you are a sinner. First John 1:9 says, "If we confess our sins, he is faithful and just to forgive us our sins, and to cleanse us from all unrighteousness." You must then realize that Jesus is the only Way to Heaven. John 14:6 says, "Jesus saith unto him, I am the way, the truth, and the life: no man cometh unto the Father, but by me." You must believe that Jesus Christ was crucified in your place and rose again the third day as the perfect Sacrifice for your sins. Romans 10:9 says, "That if thou shalt confess with thy mouth the Lord Jesus, and shalt believe in thine heart that God hath raised him from the dead, thou shalt be saved."

If you want Jesus to come into your heart and save you, then all you need to do now is pray.

EXAMPLE PRAYER: "Jesus, I know I'm a sinner. I'm sorry for the wrong I've done, and I ask Your forgiveness. I believe that You are God's Son, that You died for my sins, and that God raised You from the dead. I want You to come into my heart to save me from my sins. In Your Name I pray, amen."

"My sheep hear my voice, and I know them, and they follow me: And I give unto them eternal life; and they shall never perish, neither shall any man pluck them out of my hand. My Father, which gave them me, is greater than all; and no man is able to pluck them out of my Father's hand. I and my Father are one."

John 10:27-30

ABOUT THE AUTHOR

BORN IN BELLFLOWER, CALIFORNIA, MALANYA M. Donaho was six months old when her parents relocated to Arkansas. She was raised in a Christian home, accepted Jesus as her Savior when she was five, and was thirteen when writing found her. Upon graduating high school, Malanya entered the workforce, where at age twenty-one, she met the man God had created for her. A year later, they were married and now have two children: a daughter in Heaven and a son who has surrendered to be an evangelist. In addition to writing, Malanya loves singing, song writing, playing piano, playing video games, reading, storm spotting, and furthering her knowledge of American Sign Language. Malanya and her family attend Grace Baptist Church of Conway and live in Central Arkansas with her mother-in-law, their six dogs, three cats, and various goats and chickens, the number of which fluctuates on a regular basis.

For more information about
Malanya M. Donaho
and
Amazing Grace: A Novel
please visit:

mmdonaho1.wordpress.com
www.facebook.com/m.m.donaho
@m_donaho

Ambassador International's mission is to magnify the Lord Jesus Christ
and promote His Gospel through the written word.

We believe through the publication of Christian literature, Jesus Christ and
His Word will be exalted, believers will be strengthened in their walk with
Him, and the lost will be directed to Jesus Christ as the only way of salvation.

For more information about
AMBASSADOR INTERNATIONAL
please visit:

www.ambassador-international.com
@AmbassadorIntl
www.facebook.com/AmbassadorIntl

*Thank you for reading, and please consider leaving us a review
on Amazon, Goodreads, or our websites.*

Cece Burbin thought she knew what love was—people using you to get what they wanted. Until she met Jason Porter. But on what should have been the happiest day of their lives, Cece wakes up in the woods with a lot of pain. Jason is just as frantic to find his lost bride but struggles to trust in God to take care of her. Not realizing he doesn't have much time, Jason sets out to get some answers and to search for love's lost star.

The lives of four delightful women, a homeless teen, a rebellious son, a grieving lover who is at the bottom, a son who lost his faith, and a hired murderer are all intertwined in the aftereffects of a Category 3 hurricane thanks to a few passages written by one determined woman.

After Catherine Reed's husband dies, she moves back home in order to accept a new position as the teacher for the town's one-room schoolhouse. Samuel Harris has suffered his own loss and guilt has burdened him ever since. When his old flame comes back to town, he wonders if they can find healing together. Catherine believes anyone should be allowed to learn, but she is quick to find a town divided on that issue. As she and Samuel set out to change people's minds in a post-Civil War era, can they also find a second chance at happiness?